Primary Rubber: The Flat Tire Murders

CHARLES A. TUREK

PAGINATION

Primary Rubber: The Flat Tire Murders

Copyright ©2012 Charles A. Turek

ISBN-10: 061568811X
ISBN-13: 978-0615688114

This book is printed on demand by CreateSpace.com.

Published under the Pagination Books Imprint

www.paginationbooks.com

It is just possible that the tensions in a novel of murder are the simplest and yet most complete pattern of the tensions on which we live . . .

With most sincere thanks and apologies
to the late Raymond Chandler.

CONTENTS

This book would not be possible were it not for my loving wife, Rose. Thanks for suggesting that I try writing a detective mystery go to her alone. Her patience with the creative process is without bound, and her tolerance for my fruitless endeavors unending.

Primary Rubber
The Flat Tire Murders

Chapter One

Not enough rain or too much. The eternal lament of the Iowa farmer played across the radio like a symphony to spring. The agribusiness report on KSOY may as well have been a dirge. Either it was too wet or too dry. Too much rain meant too much production, leading to too low a price at the elevator and farms going bankrupt. Too little rain or flooding meant no production and farms going bankrupt. The weather, for Iowa farmers, was never sunny. Police Sergeant Arnie Whitaker thought about this as he listened to the ag report and looked for some reason to reconcile the farmer's carping about a dry May with the fact that the Army Corp of Engineers might have to dynamite a levy and flood farmland. Where'd that water come from? He guessed that too much water didn't translate into too much rain, somehow, and tried to dismiss it from his thoughts.

He'd been awakened by a call from his dispatcher at seven that morning, even though it was his day off. Iowa City didn't see many murders; seldom more than two a year, with the exception of a bad year here and there, and often none in a single calendar year. So two in one day were bound to start the flop sweat in city politicians, and bring up a bad taste in Arnie's mouth. Two murders in one day put him in the hot seat. As the only ICPD officer who had ever cracked a murder case, Arnie would have to put his day off on hold. The morning had dawned sunny and warm, and didn't look good either for Arnie or for the farmers of eastern Iowa.

He turned his well-worn '99 Chevy Tahoe off of Gilbert St. and headed for the lot next to the railroad where they'd built the new tire store a few years back. Although Arnie Whitaker knew he still had a good memory, he knew that he was getting far enough along in his career that other things were starting to fail: Like he was no longer five and a half feet of lean muscle, his shoulder ached after an hour qualifying a new weapon, and his blond mop of wiry hair had turned mostly gray. He tried to remember who owned the tire store, but the name Flatwood-Barside Tire & Auto under the big Trapp Tire logo didn't ring any bells. The suspicion that he was soon going to know more than anyone else on the planet about Flatwood and Barside made him shake it off and try to think of something else. Police cars parked at awkward angles already filled the lot, or at least made it almost impossible to squeeze in another vehicle. Arnie had given up his city car when he had gone all plainclothes. Nobody else on the force seemed to see the comedy in a plainclothes officer – today one wearing a fishing vest – running around town in a black and blue with the full complement of lights and a porcupine's back of radio equipment. In his Chevy, Arnie looked like just another Iowan, attitude and all.

His handheld squawked at him as he opened his car door, causing Arnie to jamb his thumb into the talk button and yell, "Yeah! Just gettin' here."

The tire store building looked about as nice as a building could get for that sort of operation, Arnie allowed. All clean, whitewashed concrete block, blue trim and a nice big plate glass window stocked with tire displays. On the east side, behind the glass, he could see the salesroom and waiting area; on the west, four service bays with large, blue overhead doors, only one of which was open high enough for a couple of uniforms to spill underneath and walk Arnie's way. Both men looked fit and prepared for action, with a full complement of weaponry holstered but ready. "Sergeant," said the taller officer as a greeting and salute in one.

"So what do we have? Flatwood with a side of Barside?" Arnie joked to break the obvious stress that showed on the shorter man's face. His name tag read Spindlethrift.

"Flatwood and, I think, a worker. Guy named Sharedream. Might be one of ours," the stressed officer answered.

Knowing that a call involving the murder of a police officer would have drawn many more men off the streets than was evidenced by the number of cars in the lot, Arnie assumed that Spindlethrift meant somebody from the few families of Illini or Ioway tribal members that still populated eastern Iowa. "I take it you didn't know his family."

The statement was a question, and Spindlethrift shrugged. "No more than you would know English lords and ladies."

Arnie didn't like to have his questions debated, but he had earned this one. Assuming that Spindlethrift knew every

3

Indian in the area would have been insensitive, at best, but it was his officer that had brought up the Indian name connection, not him. "Carry on," he ordered while heading as quickly as possible to the open overhead door. But he couldn't help thinking that some people were too sensitive for their own good. He'd have to give the patrolman a good talkin' to – another time.

On the way in, Arnie Whitaker noticed that the overhead door wasn't actually open a ways. The bottom section of the door was ripped off from the hinges on the section above it and laying to one side of the opening. The tracks on both sides were pulled away from the concrete block anchors, clear evidence that a vehicle had been used to force entry; or to make it look that way.

Inside the service bay, Arnie quickly noted the position of the two male corpses surrounded by uniforms and crime scene techs doing their jobs. The corpse dressed in a service blue uniform shirt and jeans lay on its right side with the tailbone up against a work table that was strewn with tools and partially disassembled auto parts. The position of the arms and legs seemed almost relaxed, as though the man had caught himself going down and then relaxed into unconsciousness. The other corpse, the one he assumed to be the owner Flatwood, lay flat on its back with its legs spread and, appropriately, extended flat out. The arms, too, were extended, spread and flat with the palms of the hands down on the bare concrete floor. It seemed to Arnie Whitaker that the dying man may have fallen in this position and then tried unsuccessfully to get up again. No wonder. A large screw or bolt of black metal had been driven into the man's forehead, square between the eyes. The fastener was the kind that had a washer stuck onto it near the head. Arnie noticed that the killer had done a good job of getting it far enough into the skull to seal off most of the blood flow. For a violent double homicide, this scene was unusually clean of blood. He stopped short of the yellow crime scene tape and looked around at the rest of the shop area.

Along the wall that separated the repair shop from the sales office stood a partially assembled set of heavy timber tire racks. The timber and steel components that hadn't yet been used were not knocked over or scattered, but still stacked neatly in a corner. Nothing else in the shop seemed to be greatly disturbed – nothing knocked over, no loose tools on the floor, nothing spilled. Except for the bodies, it looked like the shop was ready to open for business.

The glass door to the sales office had been propped open by leaning a used tire against it, and Sgt. Whitaker could hear muffled sobbing. He thought it was probably a family member, maybe a widow or girlfriend. "Who's in charge?" he asked to nobody in particular.

"You are." The answer came from a youngish man with thick muscles hidden in a light blue dress shirt and yellow tie. The sleeves of the shirt had been rolled up neatly and an obvious tattoo, nautical in nature, showed on the man's left arm. AME Reed Thomas grinned as he strode over to Whitaker's side displaying a rubber-gloved hand in indication that a handshake might not be appropriate. "But I made sure everybody did what you would order."

"What's the murder weapon on that one?" Whitaker asked pointing at the blue-collar corpse.

The assistant medical examiner sighed. "That one," he said in a way that emphasized he again thought Arnie was being insensitive, "is Seth Sharedream. He worked here. Probably earned even less than a cop. Hell of a thing to show up on a payday and get killed for the trouble. There's blunt force trauma to the back of the head. I'll have to take it in to

5

the morgue, but I'd bet on a tire iron. I'm having the men round up every one in the place and search the dumpsters and alleys for a couple blocks around."

"I'll make that a mile." Arnie smiled. "Okay, so I don't like to get too personal with the nearly deceased. And the other one seems obvious."

"Obvious unless you noticed the box of bolts sitting over there by the new racks. They match the one in Flatwood, but that's only part of the weapon. I don't think an ordinary man, even a man wearing gloves, could drive one of those into a human skull that deep. Not enough hand strength, and the threads on those bolts are unusually nasty. Designed to go into heavy timber, but with a pilot hole almost the diameter of the bolt. So my guess is the rest of the murder weapon is an air impact wrench."

Sgt. Whitaker nodded with an expression on his face signifying both surprise and approval. "I'll have the uniforms track down impact wrenches, too. Same radius. I gotta wonder, though, how somebody got close enough to the victim with one of those things. It would have to be plugged into the air and ready to go."

"Got any other ideas," asked Thomas.

"Not right now, I don't, but I'd like to know who's crying in the office out there."

"That would be the widow. Apparently, the two workers who discovered the scene called her first to find out what to do. She got here almost before the beat cops, but I don't think she disturbed anything."

"Time of death?"

Reed sighed. "Both the same. From the looks of the bodies, lividity and temperatures, and what the workers said about Sharedream always getting here about six and they got here at seven, I'd say that's right on the money. Sometime in the hour before seven this morning."

Reed Thomas gave the body of Danny Flatwood a long hard look that said his day's work was just beginning, and Arnie decided to leave him to it. "I'll go talk to the officers that got here just before the widow. But, with that door all messed up, I'd say we have a property crime gone bad."

The AME turned to the body without another word, and Arnie started to walk to the office only to be accosted by a slightly overweight, heavily sweating uniform. "Sgt. Whitaker?"

Arnie knew the sweating officer, Jack McDonald, as a good cop and a hell of a bowling buddy. "Hot out there, Jack?"

The jab didn't faze Jack, and he proclaimed, "All the tire irons in the immediate vicinity are rounded up, sir. None found off premises, sir. All bagged and tagged."

"Then I need you to detail somebody to find all the air impact wrenches, same drill."

"That's the thing, sir," Jack said with a funny look on his face. "That's the first thing that I thought of, since this is a tire store and those kinds of things are, well, like milk in a dairy. So I noticed right away that there were no wrenches and no air hoses."

"Locked in a tool box?"

"Nope, checked that too." Jack shrugged and shook his head. "I don't mind checking again, but I'm gonna bet we don't find any dumped within a mile radius, either."

Arnie Whitaker thought a second, then said, "Double bonus."

"What, sir?"

"They take the murder weapons with them and get to sell them. Alert our snitches at the flea markets." Then he thought again and said, "If they were here long enough to gather all the wrenches and hoses, is there anything else missing, any cash?"

"I'll get on that right away, sir."

"And I'll get on the hardest part – talking to the family."

Chapter Two

Charlie Komensky could probably have found a cheaper place to rent an office, but nothing had the snazzy ring to it like an address in Oak Brook. And if he were actually getting the kind of private investigations that he expected to get by having an Oak Brook address, that would have made sense. But he wasn't, and he'd signed a ten-year lease, so what the heck. Or at least that's what he told himself when he started thinking about it. Which he didn't very often, but he was making ends meet and there was some money left at the end of the month for beer and pizza. And a little for going out on the town with Linda.

Charlie awoke from the train-of-thought dream, and from his fitful nap seated at his desk, to realize that the railfan video he had been watching on his computer monitor had run out – probably an hour ago. He had downloaded it from the publisher that morning – a good solid excuse to get in a little railroad hobby time before diving into the pile of accident investigations that were the beer and pizza of his private eye business. West Side Investigations and Salvage, his personally chosen name for the business, made exactly seventy percent of its gross from investigations. Charlie regularly thanked God for the car dealer's license that let him make up the other thirty by dealing wrecked cars from the insurance companies and lawyers that gave him investigation business.

His Oak Brook landlords didn't like the salvage side of his business, because Charlie always had a wreck or two parked in the lot where they said he should be parking only a Lexus or a Mercedes. Not his fault, he reasoned, that they offered him free secure parking with the ten-year lease. But Charlie Komensky wasn't unsympathetic, either. He only had them drop the wrecks next to other tenants he didn't like – chief among those attorney Leonard Stotts, a self-absorbed, pretty boy ambulance chaser with a too-large advertising budget and too little regard for his clients. By contrast, Charlie had a rugged but certainly not movie-star handsome face. Charlie always dressed his short, medium weight frame in jeans and sport shirts in the summer and flannel shirts and cargo pants in the winter, and tended to cover his thinning brown hair with a baseball cap, as long as the logo was for a railroad and not a ball team. On the other hand, no amount of needling could get Stotts out of the pinstripes and color-coordinated ties, silk dress shirts and jeweled cufflinks. That the generally poor and sometimes desperate clients that hired Stotts couldn't see where their money was going puzzled Charlie in the way that evil puzzles the devoutly religious. When he ran out of ways to irritate Stotts, Charlie had to chalk it up to the way of the world.

At forty-eight, Charlie knew he was no spring chicken, or even a summer swine, but he didn't think he was over the hill yet, either. That's why he had quit his job at the peak of his career with the Berwyn Police Department, at the grade of Homicide Detective Lieutenant, for the work he did now. Charlie knew that the one good case, the one that would make him a legend, could walk through the door any day, and, when "any day" came, he didn't want to be employed by a Captain of Police who would take all the credit. That career he dropped for his "any day" case had started in the Chicago Police Department Academy and lasted there all of three years. Berwyn paid better, and there were fewer really good cops to compete with. When the chance came, he took it. The murder rate in a town like Berwyn, the "City of Homes," rounded out to about 2 per year, and Charlie had been good at it. He closed 99% of the cases, had even odds whether the perp would cop a plea or go to trial, and even at trial he batted better than most major leaguers. Then came the changes, the spike in crime, and the pressure to move up to get out of the field. He didn't like that, and Charlie certainly didn't want to become a paper-pusher in his last years as a cop.

So he took a hard look at his finances, got a loan from his longtime girl, Linda Chelwood, who ran a card and gift shop in the mall, and set up his detective agency. The first year of not being able to pay her anything back put that relationship on the rocks for the interval, but now they were better than ever. As long as he didn't drag her out on any train watching trips.

During his years growing up in the Hale Park neighborhood of Chicago, and later while on the street as a beat cop, Charlie had developed a fascination with railroads. "Who wouldn't," he would ask anyone who would listen. "We're living in the railroad capital of the world?" Even Berwyn had two of the best, the old Burlington Route, or the 'Q', now the BNSF Railway, and what used to be the Illinois

Central, crossing the old Burlington just east of Ridgeland and Stanley Avenues. Even though his parents had opted to stay in the city, he had had a lot of Czech relatives living in Berwyn when he was growing up. The interesting bridge where the IC crossed the Burlington had been a favorite walking destination in the mid-70s. And a short walk north of the city line into Oak Park got him to another fascinating railroad, the Chicago Northwestern, with the CTA 'L' thrown in on the same right of way along Lake Street.

Linda would have none of it, but she stuck with Charlie, even through the bad year, and continued after that to come in and keep his business going by doing the business things she was good at and Charlie wasn't.

Like picking this office condo and signing a lease that had clauses he wouldn't have understood if he had been to law school, which had always been on the back burner for him in some way. Eight offices, none bigger than his 120-square-foot space, shared a meeting room, a small kitchen with a fridge and a microwave, and a reception area with receptionist who answered calls and took messages. And don't forget the "executive toilet," which was where Charlie crapped when the stalls in the crapper down the hall were full. Two to four spaces were usually vacant, the only other tenant being there since February of 2007 being a young lawyer who did defense work. At least he got free Internet access, which brought him back around to thinking about the video he had just nap-missed when the phone bleeped at him.

No permission being asked, the receptionist, at least this week's version of the temps they hired for the position, squawked through the intercom, "There's a, uh, that is, a lady to see you." Charlie knew that no protocol existed, so he just sat still until the knock on his door came.

"Turn the knob and push," Charlie yelled. "Otherwise it just stays closed and you'll have to knock again."

Charlie expected either one of the insurance adjusters who assigned him business or one of the girls from the auto auction trying to get a signature on paperwork, but the poised female who walked in surprised him – what Charlie would have called a "dame." Reflexively, he stood up and offered her a chair.

"Much obliged," she said in a husky voice that wasn't Chicago.

Charlie couldn't keep himself from hesitating to take a good look at this strange but alarmingly seductive woman. Her long, blonde hair lightly curled back to just touch the silk blouse that covered her shoulders. No bangs for her, she had styled the hair to part just wide enough to feature her thin brows and full, brown eyes, her straight nose, and full lips. She had used a minimum of makeup, probably no more than the average businesswoman, rather than a seductress, but seductive was the only thing to be said at a first glance. A neat grey business skirt, wide belt, modest buckle and conservative handbag contrasted with the red platform spikes she had walked in on, and with the two-button exposure from the blouse that parted the curtain onto a view of average breasts heaving in a just-to-be-seen red push-up. Seated in his client chair with her legs crossed, she revealed more than enough smooth, white thigh to deliver the invitation.

He couldn't keep himself from thinking like a detective, either. The voice told him she wasn't from the area, or at least hadn't been there long enough to lose the country. Probably had been shopping in the mall, which was where she had bought the incongruous shoes and decided to wear them for a while. He had to admit she wore them well, not awkwardly, so she was used to some pretty radical footwear. He would have bet she had left her packages with the receptionist, but avoided the urge to check. He could check that on the way out. That she had unbuttoned number two said to Charlie that she wanted something she thought he would be reluctant to give. Nothing unusual about that, although she probably had not done any homework on him or she would know he had been with Linda for a long, long time.

Before moving behind his desk, he held out his hand. "Charlie Komensky."

"Elizabeth Wallace," she responded with a firm handshake that he thought lasted just a little too long.

Back behind his desk, Charlie folded his hands on the top in front of him and asked, "What can I do for you, Miss Wallace?"

She leaned toward him for full effect, not lost on Charlie. "Call me Liz, Mr. Komensky."

He leaned back and took his hands off the desktop. "In that case, you can continue to call me Mister Komensky until we clarify what it is that you want from me, Liz," Charlie sarcastically buzzed out the end of her name. When he was younger, maybe, but at his current age and condition? Women didn't just look at Charlie and say, "Gotta have sex with that man."

"Well, I . . . " She withdrew the approach and averted her eyes. "I guess I want nothing from you. But what I want of you is justice."

"That you can get at the courthouse, or upstairs with Mr. Stotts. I don't dispense justice, but I do solve crimes. Just what is the nature of this justice you seek?"

His new client fidgeted. For the first time she seemed less assured, less seductive. "My lover has been murdered, and I think his wife did it."

"I haven't read about any significant murders, by a wife or otherwise."

"Not here. I mean, not in the Chicago area. I'm from Iowa City." For a moment, the seductiveness vanished and Charlie's new client was just a small-town girl looking for help from a big-city cop. Then it came back with a vengeance. "I was in love with the man, Mr. Komensky. We were lovers, and I want you to imagine what that was like."

"Oh, I am," Charlie quipped. "I am."

"I mean what it was like to have my lover, the man I gave everything to, killed by a woman who meant nothing to him, and her getting away with it." A full pout ensued, followed by the story of the murders in the Flatwood-Barside tire business and Elizabeth Wallace's assertion that the cops were going to focus on two meth heads from the University of Iowa and completely ignore the fact that Flatwood's wife, Nordella, was a green-eyed bitch who didn't deserve to breathe the same air as Danny Flatwood.

Before she finished, Charlie had noticed what she wasn't telling him. Things such as how Nordella had found out about the affair, assuming the two lovebirds had been discreet about it, and how long it had been going on. She also didn't tell him why she hadn't gone to the cops with her theory, or why she was afraid to, or why they weren't listening. He did notice that she was awfully brazen about telling him details that didn't make a bit of difference, like how many times they had done it both ways in the office where Nordella shed her first widow tears. Liz Wallace either certainly had it bad for Danny Flatwood, or she had something to gain by convincing Charlie that she did.

When she paused at what appeared to be the end of the story, Charlie bluntly asked, "What's in it for you?"

Liz Wallace feigned surprise. "Why, I told you! Justice!"

"You sure you aren't second in line to inherit or something?" Charlie put on the most serious face he could muster. This dame was interesting to a fault, but hilarious in her efforts.

"Mr. Komensky!" Liz leaned forward again and stuck her rump into the back of the chair to lift her breasts. "I would do anything to see that justice is done."

Charlie smiled. "Not until I check to see that Danny didn't have any STDs. But I'll take your case." Liz Wallace visibly relaxed, but still needed to be sure she had Charlie hooked. Charlie saw this and beat her to the next question. "My fee, you ask?"

"I thought?"

"Just so we're on the same page: That was a joke about the STDs. I don't work for sex, although you may have had lovers who did." Liz looked appropriately shocked. "Ten grand retainer out of which come my expenses and $100 per hour. Ten grand is not a maximum, so you are going to have to stop me when you think I'm overspending. Is that understood?"

"Perfectly," Liz purred. The seductive voice had returned, and she wiggled her shoulders with the first syllable like a Monroe impersonator at New York, New York. "I'll see YOU in Iowa!"

Chapter Three

He'd never had such a hot potato on his hands, and Charlie Komensky knew that he had better clear the hot parts with Linda before trotting off to Iowa City. This was going to take a face to face, not just a phone call. He left instructions with the temp-slash-receptionist to call him on his cell phone only if it was an emergency, but he couldn't tell if she had unglued herself from the fan mag long enough for it to register. He needed very much not to be disturbed if this put things wrong with Linda.

On the way down to Linda's Cards & Gifts on the second level of the mall, Charlie thought he would probably soften it by telling Linda he was going to fold in a couple of days taking photos of the CRANDIC. The Cedar Rapids and Iowa City drew lots of railfans from all over the country, primarily because of having been an electric interurban until the middle of the 20th century. Linda knew that it was hard to talk him out of a trip to see a railroad, and better his mind should be on trains than on another woman. Even so, honesty was the best policy with Linda. One of the reasons they got back together after the tight squeeze on taking her loan was that he had been honest about the prospects of payback.

Linda had her back turned and was sorting greeting cards into the slots in the main display near the front of the store when he walked up. Although his libido could be stimulated by a glamorous dame like Liz Wallace, Charlie's heart never beat as quickly or as nervously as when he saw Linda. Quickly because he loved her with all of it, but nervously because commitment was something he had only done with his job. Settling down scared the hell out of him. He took in the form-fitting jeans and the cotton shirt she wore and memorized the curve of her bottom and the places he was going to put his hands when he got back. The sound of his approach made her turn, in case he was a customer, but the sight of his slightly red face and two-day beard made Linda light up. Short, but a half-inch taller than Charlie, Linda had a round face and a smile that went from ear to ear when she was truly happy. Her dirty blonde hair presented no pretense. What you saw was hers. And makeup wasn't Linda's game either. Without it, she could outshine the prettiest young actress. Charlie knew that she spent hours every night exercising to keep the slim figure and a body that presented him with formidable sexual challenges but made Charlie feel right at home. If this Liz client was a roller coaster ride, Linda was a whole amusement park.

"Wow! It's nice to see you here!" Linda said with jubilance. "What's up?"

Charlie's head was on perfectly straight, and he had no trouble telling her the whole story, even the seductive parts and the broad offer of sex in return for his services. He managed to get it all out while they were still standing there in the front of her store, and Charlie never had a harder time reading her expression that he did during that monologue. He finished with a sigh, and then said, "I'm going to call Judge Burmeister to make sure my license will be good in Iowa, and then go home to pack."

Linda reached out and caught both of his hands in hers. "And you plan to let me know you are okay every evening, right?"

Charlie nodded his complete agreement.

She grabbed his chin in her right hand and made sure he looked into her eyes, and directed, "Go then." Then she grabbed just a little too hard and dug her thumbnail into his cheek. "But if you come back with one of those STDs you mentioned," she said, smiling playfully. "You had better be ready to move the hell out of Oak Brook!"

A non-railfan could find traveling with Charlie Komensky difficult and frustrating. Charlie usually picked a well-defined route and established a reasonable itinerary, then rarely followed either. All things related to railroads tempted him away from the chosen path. An unexpected railroad yard along the way could keep him occupied for an afternoon. The promise of seeing an operating antique locomotive could take him miles out of the way. A rumor heard from another foamer – railfans are often referred to as foamers, because they foam at the mouth at the mention of a train – could keep him searching for the will-o-the-wisp train that might be the last one running on a particularly bad set of tracks that seemed abandoned to anyone else. Following an abandoned roadbed and absorbing its history, real or imagined, could take him days.

On this trip, Charlie took a detour to Galesburg, Illinois, to check out the BNSF Railway operations there, and another to Silvis, where Iowa Interstate was building a new yard for ethanol trains. But the promise of following the CRANDIC through the Iowa countryside helped limit is transit to three days, on a trip that could have been complete by eight on the evening he had spoken to Judge Burmeister. Judge Elmo Burmeister's family had employed Charlie's father after the war, and despite being a lawyer, the judge had always been a good friend. He had told Charlie that, as long as the client had come to Charlie, and as long as Charlie didn't solicit any other business in Iowa, the whole deal was good to go. And Charlie knew he could be frustratingly slow to get where he was going, so he kept calling Liz Wallace to give her an estimated time of arrival. He had just left Silvis and crossed the state line when he made the last call.

"Where the hell are you?" Her patience sounded like he had stretched it to the limit, so he made those last 75 miles in an hour and a half.

To Charlie Komensky's way of thinking, a cheap motel was either a good way to discover the underbelly of a town like Iowa City, or a good way to discover that a cheap motel is sometimes nothing more than a roach trap with a front office. He picked a place on Route 6 near the airport, a place built in the days when Route 6 had been the main highway through town and a motel included a carport for each customer, although, after trying to park his Taurus, he couldn't see how somebody could have fit a 1956 Ford into the tiny lane. That the motel also had Internet service could not have been anticipated by the customer in the '56 Ford. Even flush toilets may not have been foreseeable in 1956. The back yard had a couple of suspicious looking old sheds that probably had pits under them.

The location of the motel south of town would also keep him from being tempted to drive north and follow the CRANDIC every time he left the motel in the morning. Well, maybe not every time.

Deciding not to immediately cater to Liz Wallace's need for confirmation of his whereabouts, Komensky cracked his laptop open on the bed and searched for directions to the Iowa City PD. He found that nothing in Iowa City was more than fifteen minutes away. He also chuckled to himself when he realized that the scene of the murders was only about four blocks south of the police department. This finding could be a source of amusement during his anticipated meeting with the detective in charge of the murder investigation. So Charlie stowed the contents of his battered suitcase into the ancient three-drawer motel dresser, two drawers of which screeched so loudly when he pulled them out that Charlie was certain he had awakened bats in the next county. After a judicious application of motel soap to the bottom of each drawer, a quick shave, an organized distribution of his toilette items on the bathroom shelf, and the proper placement of his framed photo of Linda on the night table, Charlie left and drove straight to ICPD.

Knowing that Iowa City was a small town by Chicago standards, but that it was one of the largest cities in Iowa, didn't change Charlie Komensky's surprise at the size and stature of the municipal building that housed the PD, the FD, and just about every other D that the rinky-dink town needed. This was going to be harder than he thought if the city and its civil servants were delusional about their importance. Nonetheless, the drill for Charlie would be simple: Charlie would go to the front window unannounced, show his credentials, and demand to see the homicide detective in charge of the "Flatwood and that other guy murder," and then wait the appropriate amount of time in case the detective was out in the field. At the calculated moment, when Charlie knew he was being jerked around – because he had done it himself to other detectives in his day – he would demand to see the supervisor, Chief, Superintendent or Commissioner. On up the ladder he would go, to whichever title got the biggest reaction from the desk cop. He would then be assured of a reasonably quick meeting with the detective. The mood into which this little play put the homicide cop, Charlie knew, would tell a lot about where Homicide was on the investigation. If the cops had this thing nearly cleared, the detective in charge would be a lot less irritated than if he didn't have a clue.

Charlie had not been seated in one of the austere chairs – bolted to the floor – for more than ten minutes. He was just about to go into his rehearsed outrage when the door to the inner sanctum buzzed and Arnie Whitaker walked out. Far from being pissed off, Arnie had a big smile on his face and extended a hand in greeting. "Sgt. Arnold Whitaker, sir," he said pleasantly. "Always good to have more eyes and ears on the job. Particularly if our taxpayers don't have to pay for them."

Shaking hands first and then getting up, Charlie responded in his most abrasive voice, "I asked for the homicide detective in charge. Are you trying . . .?"

Arnie stopped him. "Not at all, Detective Komensky. What you see is what you get."

Charlie's eyes went wide in an expression that asked now what am I getting myself into and said, "Well, then. We gotta talk."

When they both got seated in Whitaker's office – actually a space smaller than Charlie's – Arnie Whitaker explained about how there weren't enough homicides in Iowa

City to justify the pay grade of homicide detective, and how he was the ranking officer with experience. "Of course, we can get an assist from Iowa DPS if we ask, but they're stretched pretty thin. We sometimes have to go all the way to Chicago or St. Louis or even to Kansas City for some of the crime scene analysis. But you know that." (Charlie did not.) "My judgment call was that this was an isolated case. It ain't a serial killer, if you know what I mean. And I think we can wrap this up in a week.

There it was. This cocky sergeant who had probably trained with Iowa DPS, where they trained him that the last thing they needed there was for city PDs to tie up resources on "easy" investigations, this guy thought he had the murders solved in ten days. Even Chicago PD would be hard-pressed – with their resources – for ten days. And what was this you know what I mean crap? Charlie decided to redirect the conversation. "So you had me checked out in ten minutes?"

Arnie smiled a big, ingratiating smile, and answered, "No. I had you checked out three days ago. Elizabeth Wallace told me she hired you."

Now Charlie knew he would not be able to trust anything Whitaker told him about the Wallace dame, and he regretted not having done some research on her in Chicago. "That's cozy," said Charlie with sarcasm enough to be recognized by the dumbest of cops.

"You trying to imply that Liz is a suspect?"

Charlie shot back, "Not trying to imply anything. Just implying straight out."

"She's your client."

"Okay, Sergeant." Charlie held up both hands in a gesture of mock surrender.

This just angered Whitaker more. "If we're both going to get anything out of this dance, I suggest you bring me a corsage first and take me to dinner after. Otherwise, we ain't goin' to bed."

"I said okay!" Charlie had found out more than he needed to know about Whitaker. First, that he was inexperienced, and second that he was a friend of Charlie's client. No cops that he knew would have said Liz instead of Elizabeth unless they knew the subject. "Mind telling me what you have first? You can tell me about 'Liz' later."

But Whitaker felt the need to explain. "Liz is just a friend," he stated. "And I didn't know she was heading for Chicago to hire you."

"Oak Brook. But that's another matter," said Charlie, trying to change the subject. "Tell me about the investigation, and I will decide later whether you having a relationship with my client is important or not."

Whitaker started to protest again, and then, realizing that he had been read like text on a cheap cell phone, moved on to the meat of his investigation. "Two bodies," he started. "Both victims killed by violent means and discovered at the same time in close proximity by co-workers coming to work in the morning. But it doesn't appear to be your usual workplace killing or a murder-suicide. It would have been physically impossible to self-inflict either fatal wound. Vic one, Danny Flatwood, the owner of the tire store, recently sole owner after the natural death of his partner, Tim Barside, and a probate matter that went in his favor."

"So I assume that the relative who didn't want Flatwood inheriting Barside's half is on the list of suspects?" asked Charlie.

"That would be Owen Barside, and yes, but that's not the direction I'm going."

"Only saying"

"Okay, just let me finish and you'll see what I mean," demanded Whitaker, again a little annoyed. Getting just a shrug, he went on. "Vic two is Seth Sharedream, a young man who worked at the tire store and was in the habit of coming in early to help out in return for consideration for a promotion to management. No immediate family locally. I've got some feelers out among the Indian community to see if we can come up with a next of kin.

"And I know what you're going to say," said Whitaker in a rush to get it out before Charlie hit him over the head with it. "Sharedream would have had motive if the boss nixed his promotion, but, as I said, the ME doesn't think he could have committed suicide by hitting himself over the back of the head with a tire iron."

"So you've got the murder weapons?" Again, it was a question in an assumption by Charlie.

"Uh, actually, no," admitted Whitaker. "Not the iron and not the air impact wrench used to drive a steel screw directly into Flatwood's forehead."

"And yet Elizabeth Wallace told me you are focused on two unrelated, minor drug dealers who live on the University of Iowa campus." Charlie thought about it for a moment, shook his head and asked, "How do you get to that conclusion?"

"Clear evidence of forced entry, by an MO that at least one of these dealers has used before to get money." Whitaker told Charlie about the broken overhead door.

"Forgive me for taking this in a different direction, but did Elizabeth Wallace tell you she thought you were wrong?" asked Charlie.

"I thought she was trying to protect herself."

"And well she might be," agreed Charlie. "So she's on the suspect list, too?"

"I doubt that she has the physical strength to accurately direct an air wrench with a heavy screw, but yeah, I guess so."

Charlie needed to know a few other things before he went off on his own. Like whether Whitaker was sure that the murders took place in the tire store. "ME says no sign that the bodies were moved post mortem." And like had "Arnie the Inexperienced" checked on Flatwood's immediate family and on Elizabeth Wallace's prime suspect, Nordella Flatwood.

"I don't see a motive for Nordella," answered Whitaker. Apparently "Liz" had not fessed to Arnie that she was getting her fancy tickled by Danny Flatwood. Whitaker had also checked the whereabouts of both of Danny's sons, boys ages 20 and 17, and found they had both left early to get to a ball game in Des Moines that afternoon. They had found out about their father's death when Nordella called them. "Besides," said Whitaker. "That tire business was paying for them both to go to college. The younger boy's a bit of a brain. I don't see a motive there, either."

Charlie stood up. He needed to interview Nordella before Whitaker told her about their interview, and before Elizabeth Wallace did anything else as unpredictable as she had shown herself to be so far. "Is there anything else I should know before I visit with the widow?"

"Just go easy on her," recommended Whitaker. "And, yes, there are two other angles. The first is that we haven't finished auditing the books for the business yet. Nordella gave us a little bit of a problem on that one and we had to get a court order. The other is that we found all the air impact wrenches belonging to the store out in a landfill about five miles north of here. We just don't know which wrench was the murder weapon until the tests come back."

"How do you know they belong to the store?"

Whittaker's eyes rolled up, and Charlie took that as an indication that was something the cop hadn't thought of. "We'll check their tool purchases." The statement was terse and final.

Chapter Four

The midday sun had made the inside of the Taurus hot, and Charlie opened all four windows and hoped for a breeze. He'd taken his laptop with him, but he couldn't get a Wi-Fi connection. He swore under his breath and twisted around to see if there were any coffee shops or a fast food joint nearby. Nothing.

His phone vibrated. "Hello there, beautiful," answered Charlie after noting that it was Linda Chelwood.

"So how many days did you blow train watching?" her voice answered with a question.

"Not many. How's the office?" Charlie knew Linda would have taken the first evening's opportunity to straighten out his books and his desk and whatever else she could put her feminine touches on. "Any calls?"

"You got six from InterCity Insurance asking for a bid on that '07 Chrysler. Other than that ..."

Charlie interrupted her. "Tell them four-fifty. And I need you to call one of our attorney friends that owe us a favor and have him do some digging."

"I already had my pencil ready," laughed Linda.

After telling her what he knew about Danny Flatwood and possible suspects, he instructed, "Have the attorney check to see who contested the Barside will in probate and who represented them. Whoever it was apparently lost. I don't know how much a tire business is worth, but it can't be peanuts. Then call down to CPD and get Stevens or one of his minions to check out my client. I don't think I can get a straight answer from this Whitaker cop. He ain't even a detective. So if CPD knows anything about him, it'd be a bonus. Got that?"

"It's good that I'm good with a pencil," answered Linda.

"You're good with a lot of things, baby. Just call me when you got that info." Then he realized that she had initiated the call. "Is that it?"

She had actually just called to hear that he was okay, but she said, "Just be careful of those STDs."

As far as Charlie Komensky's productivity was concerned, it would have been better if he didn't have to drive across any railroad tracks. Picking up a CRANDIC train that he could follow thirty miles out of town just made it worse. And when the crew went to beans – a railroader's way of saying they were stopping for lunch – at a roadside picnic table, Charlie wrangled a self-guided tour of the locomotive cab, as long as he promised not to touch anything. In return for this kindness, Charlie made a side trip into Cedar Rapids and bought the railroaders a cooler full of cola and a six-pack of beer "for later."

By the time he got to the modest Flatwood residence, a craftsman style beauty with a full front porch, Charlie could hear the four o'clock local newscast playing through an open front window – and just ending. A knock on the screen door and two pushes of the doorbell button got nobody to open the door. Peering into the open window, Charlie could see flowers and trays of pastry and cookies sitting on a sideboard. Probably from the wake and funeral, he reasoned. "Anybody home?" Still nothing.

It didn't seem like the kind of neighborhood where anybody locked their back gates. The neighborhood was mostly one of mature trees, older, roomy homes and side drives with garages in the back. He decided to walk around the house, but just to be on the safe side, Charlie yelled, "Visitor here. Anybody in the back?"

As he approached the back corner of the house, he started to realize that the back yard wasn't going to be what he expected. At the back of the lot, the original frame garage had been demolished in favor of a two-story carriage house with a three-car beauty on the ground level and enough living space next to it and above it that it had to be bigger than his Berwyn bungalow. A tiled patio had been installed next to the lower level living area, and a modest but well-landscaped pool and hot tub occupied the space from there forward to the back of the main house. In the shade of a deck that had been built onto the second level of the main house, Charlie saw a woman he assumed to be Nordella Flatwood seated on a full-length lounge with a drink in one hand, a book in the other, and pod-player ear buds in both ears.

Because she had no idea he was there, Charlie took the opportunity to look for anything about her that could tell him if she was a murderess. She looked to be in her late 40s, although Arnie Whitaker had said 51. The small two-piece she was wearing revealed a body that was well maintained. He guessed from the freckled skin and the reddish highlights in her dyed black hair that she tackled a few laps of the pool every day during summer, and hit the gym as often during the colder months; certainly a woman's body that could handle the heft of an air impact wrench. The side angle of her face was plain in every respect, at least what Charlie could see of it behind the frames of large, oval sunglasses. The towel at her feet and some residual wetness on the tile suggested she had lapped the pool no more than a few minutes earlier.

Charlie didn't want her to go all ape shit if he walked over to her unannounced, so he bent down, picked up a landscape pebble, and tossed it into the pool near her feet. When she looked up, pulling the ear buds from her ears at the same time, she was smiling. She greeted him with his name and held out a hand. No surprise there. It seems that everyone in town knew Charlie was coming except Charlie.

"Oh, Detective Komensky," said Nordella Flatwood, tossing the sunglasses to the foot of the lounge and revealing surprisingly clear, baby blue eyes. "Don't look so crestfallen. I have friends everywhere in town, and somebody was bound to find out you were here investigating my husband's death. Come! Sit with me!"

"I'm sorry for your loss," said Charlie as he let himself down as easily as he could into the next lounge over. The old, redwood lounges were built low to the ground and a little too hard on his old joints. He already dreaded getting up.

Nordella waived her hand listlessly as if to say this had not needed to be said. "What can I tell you about my husband that isn't already public knowledge?"

"You seem to have a lot of faith in the public," observed Charlie. "What do you think I should know?"

"Danny and I have been married for a long, long time. Would you care for a drink, Detective?" Charlie shook his head and Nordella continued, "We were, as you might imagine, comfortable with each other. Not out on the town with any regularity, romance reserved for holidays and birthdays, and not having brawls that required the police to be called, if you know what I mean. The last time we had a romantic vacation was just before poor Tim passed away. Had to cut it short. But that was only a short brawl, no cops there either.

"The boys are very protective of me, Detective, and I see one of them watching us from the top floor of the guest house back there." She gestured with her eyes, and Charlie looked over his shoulder to see a sullen teenage male with knitted brow staring back. If looks could kill.

Nordella went on, "They don't live here anymore. Danny, Jr., the one in the window, lives with the older boy, Rafe, over near the campus. They don't understand why anyone would kill their dad.

"But I guess Tim and Danny were into other kinds of business, maybe more dangerous business. Did you know that Tim had a scientific background?"

Charlie shook his head a second time, and asked, "How much do I need to know about a man who is too cold to be a suspect?"

"Don't fence with me, Detective! I've been under some stress with all this and I am trying to be cordial so you can do what you have to do and go home."

"Sorry," apologized Charlie. "Why don't you just tell me the story as it comes to you, and I'll pick up with any questions when you're done."

"Well, anyway. It doesn't matter whether he had a scientific background or made blue cheese for a living," shrugged Nordella. "The point is that Tim had discovered a formula for synthetic rubber. That sounds unimportant, but I swear to you, Detective, it is a valuable thing. Just ask anyone who knows tires what a good synthetic would be worth in today's market."

"So he didn't try to keep that from you?"

"Not at all, Detective!" Nordella's attitude was positively jovial. "It was the one bright spot in Timothy's death! Come closer and listen to me!"

Taking a conspiratorial position, Nordella leaned toward Charlie with the backs of the fingers on her left hand to the right side of her mouth as if revealing a secret not to be shared. "The formula wasn't his. Daniel and I didn't know where he got it, and he kept it a secret until his death. Oh, my husband knew about it. They were business partners, after all. But we didn't know the details until we were going through Timothy's things after the funeral. Danny spent a pretty penny to have a patent attorney verify that this formula was a complete unknown. Nothing like it on the books." She leaned back and put her hands to her hips. "What do you think of that, Detective?"

Always the detective, Charlie asked, "Did it bother you that he spent that much money."

Nordella shot him a look that said it was an unfair question, then asked, "Do you think we are broke?" She then waved her hands to call his attention to the yard, pool, and deck. "All this?"

"Doesn't matter what you got if you can't pay the bill for it," observed Charlie. Then he went right for the main course. "Did you think he was fooling around?"

"Pish! You mean with money? Danny was as frugal as they get!"

"I mean with another woman."

Nordella laughed heartily, and then theatrically dried the tear in the corner of her eye, the one that had not materialized. She fell silent for a moment, looked at a point beyond Charlie, and said, "Ah, you think I'm good for his murder." The colloquialism of "being good for" a murder rang incongruous in her studied, mostly theatrical way of speaking.

He let it go. "Are you?"

After a long pause, the sudden appearance of her oldest son at the open patio door to the guest house seemed to signal a change in her tone. "You can just leave right now, Detective!"

Rafe Flatwood quickly flapped over to their side of the pool in a pair of cheap flipflops and a baggy pair of swim shorts. He wasted no time in confronting Charlie. "I won't let you hurt my mother," he declared angrily. Nordella didn't seem to want to interfere.

Charlie stood up. The boy had a good nine inches on him, and he didn't want to get into a brawl. The kid had an unruly head of curly, course black hair that made him look like a fighter, and he probably worked out, from the looks of him. But Charlie also knew that guilty suspects sometimes got confrontational when cornered. He decided to gin up the anger and see if the boy would spill something. "Aw, did Mommy kill Daddy?" he taunted.

"What?" For some reason, it seemed impossible to Rafe that this old fart had challenged him.

Seeing his advantage, Charlie used Rafe's surprise and simply bobbed his head as if he saw someone on the direction of the other side of the pool. Rafe turned just slightly and just long enough to realize he'd been duped. That was when Charlie put all his weight against both hands and shoved the boy into the pool.

Rafe came up spitting and sputtering and splashing wildly. "You son of a bitch!" he yelled before trying to swim in Charlie's direction.

Charlie moved to the side of the pool. If necessary, he would meet the boy head on and duck him a few times to cool him off. But Nordella stopped them both. "Rafe!" she called, still seated on the lounge. "That's enough of that! Mr. Komensky was just leaving, weren't you, Mr. Komensky?" The boy stopped his splashing.

"You haven't answered my question," Charlie pointed out.

"You mean did I kill my husband or was he having an affair?"

"Either, or both."

"You may leave now, Mr. Komensky."

As Charlie turned to go, he felt a splash on his back come from the pool, but decided to be the adult in the proceedings and kept walking along the driveway back to the front of the house. He wondered if he had long enough to do a little breaking and entering and search the house before Nordella or one of the boys realized his car was still out front, then decided against it. He could always pull that one by luring them away on some pretense at a later time.

But Charlie did take a few minutes to decide where he wanted to go next, so he sat behind the wheel of the Taurus, put the ignition key on accessory, and made sure the radio was playing some soothing music. Nordella hadn't admitted to knowledge of an affair, let alone a murder, and she just didn't seem like the type who was insecure enough to need that kind of revenge. The older boy, on the other hand, was a hothead and, though probably strong enough to pull it off, not smart or experienced enough to clean up after himself. But the boy seemed to know something.

A knock on the window brought Charlie out of his thoughts. The younger Flatwood boy stood next to the passenger door. He had his brother's hair, but cut very short, and wore casual slacks and a sport shirt. Charlie found it incongruous and chalked it up to the pressure on the younger male sibling to avoid conforming to his brother's rebellious attitude. Charlie rolled down the window.

"Mind giving me a lift?" Danny Flatwood, Jr., leaned down and asked.

"You sure your mother won't mind, Junior? Charlie wanted to see if this was another assault.

"She wouldn't mind if you took me home with you. But I just need a ride to the library," Danny stated. "I'm almost eighteen, you know."

"Going on forty," stated Charlie as he popped up the button and Danny got in. "You ain't gonna get 'all up in my face,' as you kids say, are you? 'Cause if that's the case, I'd just as soon you walk."

"Are you trying to find out who killed my dad?" asked Danny forthrightly.

"That's the plan."

"Turn right up two blocks," directed the boy. "And you think my dad was doing it with someone? Behind my mom's back?"

"Let's just say that I have reason to believe that the wild monkey dance was being done." Charlie liked this boy's direct manner, so he also asked, "Do you know who it was?"

Danny shook his head no, then went silent for awhile until Charlie had made the right turn. Then he said, "If you want to find out, though, you should ask his best friend."

"Is that a woman?"

"Go up about six blocks to the light. You need to turn left there and the library will be on your left." Danny fell silent again, almost until they had reached the signal. "Just go around a few blocks and take me home. I don't need to go to the library," he finally admitted. "I don't know who my dad was seeing. If he was. But after Mr. Barside died – you know, his partner – Dad started hanging out a lot with Mr. Sheffield."

"Now we're getting somewhere," Charlie thought to himself. Then he asked, "Does Sheffield have a first name?"

"I think his name is Lincoln," Danny answered, looking like he wasn't really sure. "He runs the only chain of independent drugstores left in Iowa City. Whenever he's over for dinner, all he talks about is something he calls the 'Waltopus.' I think he means the big chains taking all his business away. He's always talking about getting an investor who could give him enough money to go statewide."

"Could that be your dad?"

"Dad spent all his money on the tire store. And on making Mom happy." The boy looked sullen.

"I heard you're going to college." This was a fishing expedition for Charlie. He wished that the police audit of the tire store had already been completed, so he added, "Or was somebody just blowing smoke."

I got accepted," Danny shrugged. "Dad said he knew he'd have the money and there would be no problem."

"What about Rafe?"

"Rafe's a goofball. He ain't gonna finish no matter how many years he goes. He told me himself that he just wants to ride the money until somebody figures out he should be working for Grandpa. It's one of the reasons I live at his place. Dad thought I was the responsible one and wanted me to keep an eye on him." Once again, Danny looked sullen.

Charlie turned another corner, and they were almost back to the curb in front of the Flatwood house when he asked, "Do you think Rafe killed your Dad."

They came to a stop. Charlie half expected the boy to get out without answering the question, but he just sat there for a few moments, and then said, "I'll vouch for him, if I have to. But my brother's a goofball, not a murderer. He talks up a big story, but can't get it up when duty calls." Danny opened the door, but sat still for almost another minute. Charlie tried to read the kid's expression, but it had gone off somewhere into another universe.

"You better go, kid. I don't want to have to throw your brother in the pool again." It was an unnecessary dig that Charlie regretted the minute he said it.

Danny started to get out, and then stopped with one foot out the door. "In case you're wondering, I have my own alibi."

"Yeah, I know. Baseball game in DesMoines."

Danny shook his head. "I mean a real one. Dumb cop didn't even check the game schedule. I was with this girl that Rafe sees. He invited her over the night before they found my dad, but he wasn't there when she got there. We hit it off and I got her number." Danny recited the phone number and told Charlie her name was Gloria. He slammed the door and started walking up the driveway before Charlie could thank him or point out that he hadn't really answered his question about Rafe.

Charlie decided that anyone who offered up an alibi without being asked just made that person more of a suspect. When it came down to it, the kid had gone out of his way to finger his brother. He'd have to check out the college bimbo, and decided that college must be decidedly different than it used to be if a kid like Danny Flatwood, Jr., could get a college girl to sleep over that easy. Ignoring his own admonition, he didn't drive away, but instead picked up his cell and dialed Linda to see what she had.

He wasn't disappointed, and it made him remember another reason why he liked Linda: She was a good investigator. He had asked her a few questions and she had picked up the ball and run with it. Not to a touchdown, but within punting distance. Linda told him that she had dug up information on his client, as well as on Sgt. Whitaker and Nordella Flatwood. In addition, she had been on line watching the local news from all three network affiliates in Iowa City.

She started with Nordella, who she had found was once Nordella Harding. Her father was Bicklin Harding, age somewhere in his 70s depending on where you looked, who had been born in Indianapolis but made his fortune in agricultural products in Iowa. Her mother, also still living, was Becky Harding, and she had been a member of an even more wealthy Iowa family, the Raglans of Sioux City. In any event, there was no shortage of money in the Harding family, so Linda saw that as a strike against Nordella murdering for money. "Of course, there's always passion," Linda observed suggestively. Based on a quick asset check, it was unlikely that Nordella had anything more than a wife's financial interest in the tire business.

After Charlie asked her to check if any patents had been filed in her name or in the name of the deceased Mr. Flatwood, Linda moved on to Liz Wallace. "Your client," she said, emphasizing the word client to show disdain, "was once Elizabeth Harding. Not a sister, but a cousin on Bicklin's side of the family. So I would expect she has no shortage of money, either."

"What's she got against her family that we don't know about?" Charlie asked.

"Nothing I could find," answered Linda. "But she throws her influence around just as well as the Hardings do. Maybe even better than they do. You know that I always look for clues in what kinds of lawsuits a family is involved in. Just like you taught me."

"So what did you find?"

"Of the sixty-seven lawsuits brought by members of the Harding family in the past ten years – at least the Hardings we know about – she was responsible for thirty-seven of them. And," Linda continued, "she's not even on a token board of directors. I wouldn't cut across this broad's path, if I were you. I wouldn't even walk down the same path unless you were carrying her bags and she was about to give you a big tip. By the way, where's the money?"

Charlie had to chuckle at Linda's concern. He had been involved with litigious clients more than once in his career, and he wasn't scared by the inside of a courtroom. "Apparently in the Harding family, from what you tell me," Charlie answered flippantly.

"No. I mean where's the retainer?"

As his eyes plead to an imaginary heaven somewhere in the headliner of his car, Charlie remembered that Linda had the security password to his bank account. Leaning on clients for money was not something Charlie usually did until he was sure they were no longer suspects. But he played stupid. "You mean she hasn't wired it yet?" He knew he hadn't asked her to.

Realizing she had gotten caught checking on his finances, Linda first went on the offense. "You'd be broke if it weren't for my snooping," she pointed out.

"Who said the word snooping?"

"I mean, no, no she hasn't," Linda blubbered. "Do you want me to call and play accounts receivable?"

"I'll handle it." Just as Charlie said this, he saw the strobes from a police vehicle pull up behind him. "Damn that woman."

"Who?" asked Linda, "miss STD?"

"No, the suspect I just talked to. I think her son called the po-po."

"Go do what you gotta do. Talk later." Linda's end of the connection went dead.

By this time, the cop had already opened his door and got out. Charlie could see in his outside mirror that it was Sgt. Whitaker, and he rolled down the window and said, "Afternoon, Sergeant."

Whitaker leaned in, gave the inside of Charlie's beat up interior a once over, and then looked Charlie in the eye and said, "I just want you to know that I'm not here to bust you. But you may have found out by now that Nordella Flatwood's family has a bit of political influence around here, so it wouldn't look too good if we didn't respond to a call about a suspicious vehicle in front of her house."

Charlie chuckled, then observed, "Looks like your friend Liz, her cousin, also likes to throw her weight around."

"She's your client."

"It won't be necessary for you to keep reminding me of that. And she won't be if she doesn't pay me," said Charlie.

"It'll probably be with some of the money from my settlement," guessed Sgt. Whitaker. "She sued me and the department for a little incident on campus a few years back."

"So that's how you know her?" Charlie stated it like a known fact to see if he'd get an objection.

But Whitaker changed the subject. "We got a print off one of the air wrenches and we're probably making an arrest as we speak," he stated. "Hate to cut you off, but if you don't get paid soon you probably won't. If you want to follow me to the station, you can sit in on my interrogation of the suspect.

Later that day, as Charlie Komensky drove back to his motel from the police station, he couldn't get one thing out of his mind: Sgt. Arnie Whitaker hated college students. During the course of the interrogation of suspect Jason Littleton, a sophomore from Milwaukee, the policeman had let fly just about every petty thing that he thought was wrong with college students. Among them were that they were dirty, ill behaved, cost more than their share of the local police budget, they were sexually immoral and prone to do stupid things, their habitats were rat's nests, and their penchant for drinking beer just plain disgusting. "Why would anyone," he had asked the suspect, who had been brought in to the station in handcuffs and wearing nothing more than worn blue jeans, a pair of cotton sox, and a T-shirt that said something like OMFUG. "Why would anyone let their daughters show their breasts to slime like you just to win free beer in some kind of perverted bar contest?"

Wincing at that, Charlie had tried not to watch Whitaker, who was heated, and had watched the suspect instead. He had seen mostly a blank stare, but it became one of incredulity when Whitaker started in on the morals stuff, sort of like asking what cave mother spawned this crazy cop. Just when Charlie had thought the cop was going to go change into his white robes and pointy hood, Whitaker had paused, taken a breath and asked a clerk to bring in the file.

Charlie had been waiting for the opportunity to look over the police file and had hoped he could do so while Whitaker had distracted himself with his unreasonable anger at this pipsqueak of a suspect. While Whitaker shot the usual and unusual questions at the boy, and tried to tear apart the answers, Charlie had put his hand on the file jacket and slowly slid it in his direction on the table. The first thing he had noticed was that the physical evidence consisted of a single fingerprint, smudged but conclusive, and no DNA to match to the suspect, who had a previous arrest for petty shoplifting. Without a confession or an eyewitness, that wasn't going to be enough to make murder stick. A warranted search of the kid's dorm room had been done, but neither the tire iron nor anything that appears to have been stolen from the scene had been found. The kid had two credit cards in his wallet, both his father's, and otherwise had about sixty dollars in cash between the wallet and a desk drawer. No drugs had been found, no doubt much to Sgt. Whitaker's dismay.

So Charlie had asked himself what evidence the file contained that did not point in the direction of Whitaker's pipsqueak. The autopsy that had been completed on Danny Flatwood was clean for drugs and alcohol, for any major health problems, and for STDs. Charlie chuckled at the thought of this ruling out Danny and Liz Wallace being lovers. Arnie Whitaker shot him a glance that told Charlie to be serious, but Charlie was sure the cop thought Charlie was laughing at one of the suspect's lame non-answers to questioning. When he was sure that Whitaker had again lost himself in his harassment of the suspect, Charlie turned the page to the Sharedream autopsy. Also clean for drugs and alcohol and for any major diseases, but lo and behold, AME Thomas had found traces of dried semen in a location that made it clear the victim had not been having normal sex at the time. Almost certainly, this ruled out the pipsqueak as a suspect, but relit the flame under victim number one's wife and society matron Nordella Harding-Flatwood.

By this time, Whitaker had moved on to threatening the complete ruin of the pipsqueak's life and the life of anyone who ever loved him. The volume level from both the cop and the suspect became so loud in the small interrogation room that Charlie had put an idea in play. Glancing at one more page, a page that stated with certainty that no fingerprints had been found on any of the other tools or on the screw that had penetrated Flatwood's cranium, he had gotten up, quickly gathered the paperwork of the file into the folder, and stepped to the doorway. "Sgt. Whitaker wants a copy for the suspect's lawyer, pronto," was all he had needed to say. Before Whitaker had known the file was gone, Charlie's "lawyer" copy had been tucked snugly into his waistband.

Taking quick leave had been easy: Whitaker hadn't noticed Charlie was leaving. Driving home on the country road at a little before sunset, Charlie wondered if Whitaker would kick the crap out of the pipsqueak before releasing him. He had to release him, didn't he? After all, the evidence said that the suspect didn't do it.

Charlie had cleared town and was southbound on the way to his hotel. No doubt about it: The growing season and an Iowa countryside had its charms. Long yellow streaks of light and shadow crossed the road ahead of him as he passed a stretch of tall poplars that bordered a water-filled ditch on his right. Wide enough and deep enough to breed fish, the ditch had lured at least one country fisherman, who was just packing up his rod and tackle box as Charlie drove past. The air was so clear that day that Charlie could see the exact moment when the sun went below the horizon, and the light lessened appreciably. Charlie turned on his headlights and adjusted the radio, but all he found was a station playing country classics. "All I got to show is blisters and sweat," sang Joe Diffie.

The Hummer came out of nowhere. Charlie had been to more "evasive driving" classes than most former cops, and it still took him longer to react than it should have. The big black vehicle must have pulled off of a side road from behind the row of trees, but, in the dim light, Charlie hadn't noticed where that road must have crossed the wide, water-filled ditch. The passenger-side corner of the Hummer grazed the passenger side rear bumper of the Taurus in a way that just gave Charlie momentary loss of control. He reacted by getting the Taurus stabilized in the lane and accelerating from the threat.

He checked his inside rearview and saw the Hummer stabilizing itself, having made a wide right turn that involved spitting gravel from the east shoulder and leaving volumes of rubber smoke over the road behind it. As it approached him, closing the gap quickly at what was now a clip of 85 per, the brights went on. This coupled with the dim light and the lift of the big four-wheeler prevented Charlie from seeing who was driving. A little more pedal brought him to 90 while Joe Diffie sang over the radio. Charlie knew this was a no-win situation.

Either somebody wanted Charlie out of the way, or somebody saw him take the file. The third, and maybe equally plausible explanation for this assault could only be a redneck joyride and some clean fun at the expense of the old car with out-of-state plates. But doubt as to the motivation faded from Charlie's head as the first nudge almost sent the loose rear end of the old Taurus toward the centerline. "When you're down in a ditch in the Tennessee sun," twanged the radio. Charlie knew this guy wanted him to roll over at high speed.

"Okay, buddy. I just need a little time," said Charlie out loud. He pulled his police .38 out of the glove box and secured it in his waistband, then made sure he could unlatch his seatbelt as quickly as possible. He looked up into the mirror and saw the Hummer approaching for another nudge. Countering it this time by accelerating slightly before the impact, doing 93 now, Charlie thanked God that he carried a couple of waterproof plastic evidence bags under his seat. One would be large enough to protect his laptop computer and the file copy he had taken from Whitaker. He hoped he could drive with his knees until he could get the bag filled and before the next assault.

With little time to spare, Charlie pulled the seal on the bag and threw it into the back seat. He would let himself be run off the road, but he wasn't going to let himself be killed in the process. The third impact was harder than the first, and as if the driver of the Hummer had anticipated his thoughts, the impact came from the driver's side rear, making the Taurus hunt toward the middle of the road; not the direction Charlie wanted to go. But he got his hands back on the wheel and accelerated one more time. Though the light was getting dimmer, he could see that there was a slight hill about a half mile ahead, and the opportunity for what he had planned would end once he got there. It would have been nice to have a bigger vehicle on his side – with his driving skills he could most certainly have run the Hummer off the road then – but he did not, and had to make do with the tools he had.

Driving with his knees again, Charlie grabbed a second evidence bag, scooped up as much air as he could and pulled the seal again to make an air-filled pillow. It wasn't very big, he told himself, but it would do. He had three seconds before the next impact and maybe fifteen or twenty before the ditch on his right ended in a dogleg to the right to follow the hill. One, two, three, he hit the brakes, steered to the right, and drove into the ditch just as he felt the whack at the right rear of the Taurus. Let the murdering bastard in the Hummer think he had caused Charlie to go into the water.

The Taurus cut into the deep ditch at an angle and sliced the water like a knife, going down until the water was about at the back window, then bobbing back up again so that the water was lapping over the hood at the windshield wipers. The engine had already drowned on the water intake, and Charlie needed the Taurus to sink to the bottom, and fast. He already could see that the Hummer had come to a stop about fifty yards ahead and was backing up. Charlie again thanked God, this time for window cranks in cheap cars – no doubt an electric window would not work now. The Hummer came to a stop, and Charlie ducked his head under the water that now filled the cabin of his Taurus up to his armpits. Then, emitting a belch from the rear, the air in the trunk exhausted and the car went down at the stern; that is, if a Taurus could have a stern and not just an ugly rear end. Charlie held his breath, prepared to breathe from the air pillow if needed.

The complete darkness under the water made the after-sunset sky seen through the water's surface from above seem bright to Charlie. He could make out the dark shape of the Hummer, and the equally dark shape of a single person walking around the front of it to look down at him. The person seemed to be holding a long gun, a shotgun or a rifle maybe. About 30 seconds in, Charlie took a draught from the air pillow. The good news was that the bubbles from his exhalation just mingled with the bubbles from the car interior – a whole lot of urethane foam letting go if its gases. The bad news was that the air pillow deflated a lot more than he had hoped on just one breath. How persistent would his would-be murderer be? Or was this just a warning? Was the light that he saw bright enough to illuminate the Taurus, and Charlie along with it?

But the rifle, or whatever it was, stayed pointed down and to the left of the figure. Seconds passed that seemed like an eternity, and Charlie had to tell himself to stay focused and

take another sip of air. This time, the bag deflated completely.
With what he had, Charlie would have to be ready to propel
himself to one side or the other, far enough from the focus of
the figure – at least he assumed the spot where the Taurus had
gone under was the focus – so that he could surprise the
figure, take a breath, and dive again before the figure could
get off a shot. If that thing's a shotgun, Charlie told himself,
that wouldn't be such a hot idea.

The car's interior fittings had just about finished
blowing off gas, and Charlie knew that to exhale then
wouldn't just tell the figure he was alive, but also pinpoint his
location. Just when he was ready to spring through the
window and swim as far in the direction opposite to the
business end of the rifle, the figure nonchalantly pointed the
gun upward and turned to go back around the front of the
Hummer. Just give it a few seconds, Charlie told himself over
the sound of this heart both beating deafeningly in his ears
and trying to burst from his chest at the same time. The sound
of the big cleated tires of the Hummer grabbing for dirt and
traction came through the water just fine, though, and Charlie
kicked upwards, broke the surface and breathed. He could
see the taillights disappearing in the direction they both had
been going.

Not wanting to lose track of the whereabouts of his car
under the murk, Charlie dived again and managed to find the
bag with the file and his gun. Good thing about a gun, it had
been enough weight to keep the bag from moving from the
back seat, even as the good ship Taurus had gone under and
the car's radio had gurgled its last strains of Joe Diffie. "When
you're down in a ditch it's a son-of-a-gun."

Identifying a goddamn almost-but-not-nearly-quite
military vehicle with the Taurus paint on its front bumper

shouldn't be a difficult project in a town the size of Iowa City. That's what Charlie kept telling himself on the walk – about three miles – to his motel. He had to think about something, because the mosquitoes and black flies were driving him crazy, and his Hush Puppies, soaked as they were, had taken on definitely sinister characteristics that spelled havoc for his bunion and general pain for the soles of both feet. He tried to stay out of the headlights of passing cars, and watched diligently for the sinister shape of the black Hummer. Who knew if the guy – he was reasonably sure it had been a guy – would patrol the road in case Charlie had survived? And swatting at the mosquitoes at the wrong time would just net him a ride as a hitchhiker – something he didn't want so long as it was somebody he didn't know or trust. There could be others out there looking for him. And having Whittaker arrest him for pointing a gun in the nose of a good Samaritan wasn't an option either. "Hello, Linda. I've been arrested for assault with a firearm and for stealing files from the police. Hello, Linda? Linda?" Yeah, that would go over real good.

Something told Charlie that the best thing to do was just walk to the motel, order up some calamine lotion from the front desk, and try to keep from scratching until he fell asleep. Nothing complicated about that. Something also told Charlie that that scenario wasn't going to fly.

The first clue he was right hit him as he walked into the courtyard of the motel. Cars filled every parking spot in the place, including the spot reserved for his now ditchwater-pickled Taurus. He shrugged it off a bit, just as he swatted a few flies that had homed in on him from the trash bin next to the picnic table. After all, it was almost summer. Or maybe it was summer – had Memorial Day passed yet? Charlie relied on Linda to keep track of those things. In any case, whether it was the height of the travel season or not, Charlie had his room key, and what did he care if somebody used the space tonight. He didn't need it. And he'd have a rental car soon enough tomorrow – mental note: Order rental right after calamine lotion. He could think about letting the air out the tires of any poor sucker who tried this again tomorrow, unless he solved the case before then.

Charlie obliviously inserted the key into the lock and turned, and the door swung open to reveal all of the lamps turned on. On the bed, which had been turned down for sleeping, Charlie saw an envelope packed with money lying on top of what looked like steno paper with a pencil-written note. The room appeared to be empty, although the door to the bathroom was closed and Charlie couldn't remember whether he had closed it before leaving. No matter, housekeeping could have done it, same way they turned down the bed. But the cash?

Charlie tossed the now dry bag with the laptop and file onto the bed and put his hand on his .38. His wet leather belt resisted a little as Charlie tried to make the weapon free for the draw. Moving closer to the bed, he could see the signature on the note. Liz.

Damn woman! He'd told her to just transfer the money into his account. Now Linda would have to deposit cash and answer all those dumb IRS questions. "Damn," Charlie said aloud. Tucking the .38 back into his waistband – probably shrunken a few sizes – he picked up the note.

It read, "Dear Charlie Komensky: I thought you'd enjoy it more with the lights on."

In one well-practiced move, the detective dropped the note, pulled the .38, and whirled, while pulling back on the hammer, to face anything or anyone that could have followed him into the room. Nothing. The he whirled again at the sound of the bathroom door coming unlatched, and Liz

Wallace walked into his gun sight. Not so much walked as insinuated. Completely without a stitch of clothes and wet from the shower – his shower, and probably using his fresh towels – Elizabeth Wallace struck a slightly obscene, definitely aggressive and boldly suggestive pose in the doorway. An impressive piece of feminine work, Charlie had to admit. Whether everything was real or the artwork of a particularly adept plastic surgeon, it all fell into the right places, and Charlie used his aimed gun as an excuse to take inventory. The feminine neck, itself quite smooth and without flaw, landed lightly on a set of shoulders that lifted just the right, balanced number of breasts with both nipples pointing in the right direction. Almost a boxer's set of abdominals showed on a slim tummy, and where the gun sight went next, Charlie found an interesting, and at the same time obscene tat pointing to where some good waxing had cleared the brush from the front gate, so to speak.

"Looking or shooting?" asked Liz as though there wasn't really a loaded gun pointed at her lady parts.

Charlie took a second to let the hot legs that held up all the rest burn into his memory, then yelled something at Liz that she didn't understand. "Linda Chelwood!"

"What?"

"You heard me. Remember that name! She's my girl. And if you think you're the first client to try something like this with me, well, you'd be right. But it ain't gonna happen. 'Cause if it did, Linda would empty all six rounds from this gun into that nice little tummy of yours without flinching." He slowly clicked the hammer forward, dropped the safety on, and threw the gun onto the bed. "Besides, you wouldn't like the swelling on my back, the chiggers on my legs, and it wouldn't surprise me if there were a half dozen leeches under my pants. So back off."

Liz shrugged as though it wasn't any big deal, an expression of attitude that Charlie would remember later. She made a model's runway turn back into the bathroom, and Charlie sat on the edge of the bed. In no more than a minute, she came back out fully dressed in a pair of tight jeans and a white, silk blouse. A pair of sandals with a bit of heel on them and a gold choker rounded out a complete wardrobe that looked as though she had taken days to get it on. Charlie, by this time, had made a wet spot on the throw. He was in misery, and he needed badly to get into that tub and take a hot bath without worrying about what his client might do with the information he carried.

"Look, Miss Wallace, I don't want you to get the wrong idea," he started.

"I understand," Liz huffed. "You've had a bad day, and you look like hell. All dressed up and you don't want to go the places I do. Okay, Mr. Detective, I understand. Your girl gets it up for you and I don't. No problem. I'll see you around town. Don't spend all my money in one place."

Chapter Five

The hot bath fixed the insect bites and the other assorted problems that Charlie had with his aging muscles and joints, but it didn't help him sleep. For more hours than he wanted to be awake, he pored over the police files that he had saved from drowning. Where the autopsy results went into intimate detail, and there had been no question that the large bolt had caused enough cranial damage to be the cause of death, it still bothered Charlie that the murderer was somehow able to approach the victim, chuck up the bolt, and bury it into the victim's skull before the victim could evade the attacker. Had the victim been otherwise occupied? The AME stated with some certainty that the victim had fallen after being "screwed", and that the other marks and bruising on the body were consistent with a fall from an upright position. There had been no signs of prior restraint.

Danny Flatwood didn't get screwed lying down! This thought made Charlie curse his warped sense of humor, and then excuse it by remembering that he'd probably be in a mental hospital by now if he couldn't laugh these kinds of brutalities off with some dark humor. He remembered the time a Berwyn hooker had literally screwed her john by crucifying him to a headboard. Not such fatal results, but still bloody and brutal, nonetheless.

Charlie drifted off to sleep about four, and then didn't get up until nine, when the sun was already recycling the night's humidity back into the grasshopper-filled air of a rural Iowa summer morning. He awoke with a headache and an all too vivid recollection of a repeating nightmare in which he had been surrounded by black Hummers and had demanded, over and over, the name of the silhouette with the rifle. That and the car rental guy pounding on his door to deliver the Mustang he had ordered on the rental website. No rest for the wicked, or at least Linda would think him wicked for even taking a good look at Liz Wallace's nether parts. The devil and STDs, and God bless the Internet.

He managed a quick, disinterested shave, followed by too many ounces of Old Spice on too many raw insect bites, and then by – according to the label – too many tablets of Tylenol. He threw on a T-shirt over black slacks and then thought about whether he should carry his gun with him or just in the glove box. He chose the latter, but threw on a heavier summer flannel shirt over the T.

No amount of morning whiskey was going to help, so he decided that he would try to find a pancake house on the way to the tire store; someplace where he could get enough protein and carbs to counteract the fatigue from the night before.

Nobody carried cash these days, but Charlie had to. He still had his wallet, somewhat wet, and used a credit card for the rental. Damn that Liz! He'd probably have to stop at a men's store in town and see if they still sold money belts. Halfway to town, he passed the spot where his Taurus slept with the fishes and realized he needed a cell phone. He had to drive through town all the way to the Interstate, where he found a Denny's in a truck stop that sold throw-away cell phones and bought one with a hundred-minute card. He called Linda, left a message when she didn't pick up asking what he should do with ten grand in cash, and then he called the motor club and told them it would be a difficult tow, but he expected them to stick to the deductible, no questions asked. Last but not least, he ordered the trucker's breakfast and downed the whole thing in fifteen minutes.

What he had expected and what he saw when he got to the tire store turned out to mesh like the gears on a '56 Ford. Danny Flatwood's heirs apparent had wasted no time in getting their feet wet in the tire business. The older Flatwood boy stood at the side of the parking lot giving directions, while a sign company guy in work overalls used a bucket crane to carefully remove the Barside name from the rectangle under the brand logo, to replace it, Charlie supposed, with the name Nordella. Although the boy glared at Charlie, he didn't try to stop the detective from going inside.

Charlie knew that he was too late to treat this as a crime scene, but just getting the smell of the place, the feel of the grit on the floors, and the rhythm of the business operation would tell him something. He noticed right away, for instance, that all the service bays were full and that there were a number of technicians diligently working, not just standing around or wondering where to put their tools. This business didn't get this way since the wife took over. And these people weren't recent hires. They knew their jobs. Danny Flatwood had run a tight and efficient ship, with loyal employees who would stick around to help the family in their moments of distress.

He observed Nordella Flatwood at the counter of the sales office with a man he didn't recognize, but who seemed to be a salesman of some sort. In the back office, he could see at least two clerical people working with concentrated intensity at their computer screens. He took a chance and wandered into the back, but neither Nordella nor Rafe seemed to notice. Off in one corner of the rectangular and very cramped office, Charlie discovered a third clerical person cranking out what appeared to be the better part of a roll of paper tape from an adding machine. The woman with long, red hair had her back to Charlie and appeared to be working from paper records rather than from the computer. As hunched over her work as she was, Charlie found it hard to gauge her age. He would guess middle age, as her flower print blouse, conservative brown skirt, and nurse's shoes suggested.

"Pardon me," Charlie said after walking just behind her ratty office chair. "Are you the forensic accountant?"

"Nope," she answered, and her fingers kept entering numbers in such a way that the little machine produced a continual whiz and an almost constant flow of tape.

"I'm sorry, but I would have thought."

The woman's right hand froze over the keys of the adding machine, and its whizzing stopped. "Listen, buster, whoever you are," she spat. "Have you ever tried to add six months of ledger figures with some asshole yammering at you?"

"I thought."

"You didn't think, did ya?" she declared. Then she twisted back in her seat to let Charlie see a homely face about his age punctuated by two light blue eyes that twinkled with mischief. "Well, ain't you the hunk, Charlie Komensky!"

Charlie couldn't believe his eyes as she got up, and he hugged her tightly. "The last time I saw you was in a basement office at CPD trying to clear that evidence room scandal! What was it, Aggie? Maybe eight years ago?"

"That was fourteen years, Charlie Komensky. So I thank you for not making it longer." Aggie's standing height was the same as Charlie's, so she could look him straight in the eye. "How'd you get mixed up with this piece of shit?"

"Still as foulmouthed as ever." Charlie shook his head and added, "First tell me what's going on with Doug."

Douglas Christie had been on CPD for most of the years that Charlie had been with Berwyn Police. Doug and Charlie had collaborated a couple of times, but Charlie had worked more with Agatha. Agatha Christie had always been able to sniff out a financial fraud where others saw only neatly added columns of numbers, and the name coincidence had never been lost on Charlie either. She had the imagination of a mystery writer.

But Aggie had bad news. Doug had caught a slug in the knee and had developed a bad infection – one of those flesh-eating things – and Aggie was taking on extra commissions in order to make ends meet. It didn't look good for Doug, who, at best, would lose the leg.

"Now I'm going to have to drop by and see him when I get back to the big city," Charlie promised, hoping to find an opportunity to change the subject. As long as he had been a cop, and then a freelance detective, Charlie had never gotten over the impulse to avoid the subject of getting hurt on the job. Intellectually, he knew that there was always the possibility – yesterday afternoon could have been his last. But emotionally, Charlie just couldn't cope with the reality of it and the effect it had on the friends and family of the fallen officer. He hoped, if it happened to him, Linda would just tell his friends that he died doing what he loved doing, and that should be that. Dump the remains in the canal and move on.

"You didn't answer my question." Aggie's voice brought him out of the gloom.

"I suppose I'm in this one for the money, too. It's not often that ten grand walks through your front door and begs you to take the case." Charlie rolled his eyes as though he'd rather it hadn't.

"Well, the ten grand sure didn't come from this place," observed Aggie.

"You've always had interesting slants on cases, Aggie," he responded. "Tell me what you can."

"Well, first off," she started. "That ten grand didn't come from here. This guy Flatwood had all his accounts bunged up in this fancy computer system from Trapp Tire. Paid a pretty good bump in the franchise fee for it, and for my money you could flush it down the toilet and go back to an abacus and you'd be better off. Had to bring in a guy from their home office just to dump the accounts into a hard format. And it still wouldn't surprise me if the 'home office' was skimming off the franchise even after the big bump."

Charlie jerked his head toward the door to the sales office. "That guy talking to Nordella?"

"Yeah. Guy's name is Gromer, if you can believe it. Gromer Frederickson. Regional Sales VP for Trapp Tire. I do know that Flatwood owed the guy seventy-five on a personal note. Unless it's in the will, it's going to be hard for him to collect from the estate. So he's got to be good to Nordella. God knows what other side deals Frederickson's got going. Loaning a business associate money on a personal note isn't exactly illegal. It just smells like it is when that same business is responsible for both the income on both sides of the loan."

"Seems like I ought to talk to him," Charlie observed. "What else?"

"Not a whole lot of anything. The business was profitable enough, even though it took a hit when the partner kicked the can. Retail and wholesale was done on credit cards or commercial billing arrangements, and Danny had a whole lot of tax exempt customers to fall back on for tax purposes. It kind of gives the big lie to the theory that this was a robbery gone bad."

"Not necessarily," Charlie corrected. "Not if the general public – read that the sleaze factor – didn't know that."

"That's what I thought, until I came across a write off for a burglary that occurred at the business just before the partner cashed in his marker. When I looked into it, I found out that the business made a big point in letting the community know the burglar was wasting his time. Made it an advertising gimmick for awhile. Like, if you want to deal in cash, it's okay with us, but we prefer trusting our customers and giving them credit."

"How'd that work out for them."

Aggie shrugged one shoulder. "I didn't see any benefit one way or the other. Just saying that the sleaze factor should have known they weren't going to find a safe full of cash here."

The two clerks seemed to be getting interested in the conversation – both looking Charlie's way – so he moved closer to Aggie and lowered his voice. "So bottom line me."

Aggie looked him straight in the eye and said, "The bottom line is a few hours work away, but I can tell you nothing is missing and there's nothing hinky in the books -

with the possible exception of that seventy-five grand note. If Flatwood owed somebody else money, it isn't showing up. After that few hours, I'm catching the next bus back to Chicago and I ain't lookin' back."

Charlie said his goodbye to Aggie and assured her he would stop up and visit Doug, even though he knew he would resist doing that unless Linda somehow got wind of Doug's distress. He wanted to introduce himself to this Gromer Frederickson and see if he could navigate the guy's manure pile. All sales people had one, and Charlie expected that, with a title of Veep, Frederickson's pile stunk to high heaven.

As he moved out into the sales office, Charlie had the misfortune to look out the front window and see Liz Wallace's car parked in the lot right next to the Mustang rental. "Geez," Charlie said in a reflex he regretted but figured he'd probably have just about every time he ran across her, after last night.

"Beg pardon?" Gromer Frederickson turned from the counter where he'd been talking to Nordella and held out his hand. "I don't think we've been introduced." Frederickson was wearing a yellow golf shirt and pair of coordinated slacks from Nordstroms and a pair of custom made shoes that reflected his status. He had an impeccably manicured head of wavy hair and could have been a Hollywood stereotype for the executive who closed all his deals on the eighteenth hole – Michael Douglas, but without the cleft. Gromer's smile did its level best to lure Charlie into the snare with a set of teeth that had been whitened and straightened beyond any semblance of normalcy.

Charlie accepted the shake and excused his outburst. "I was just marveling at the efficiency of this operation," he covered.

"Yes, pretty impressive," Gromer agreed. "But this isn't my biggest vendor, or my most efficient. We've got a couple of guys in Des Moines."

Charlie interrupted him before the talk got into the part where he and the salesman would be having a dick-length competition. "I'm Detective Charlie Komensky, and I'm investigating the murder of your 'vendor,' Danny Flatwood. So I'd like to ask you a few questions."

Frederickson smiled again. "Oh, my, yes! A real private eye, eh? Well, well. Do you have a card, sir?"

Whipping his still-soggy wallet from his back pocket, Charlie flipped open the window with his PI identification. Putting it in front of the salesman's face, he stated, "That's all I got."

"Bare bones, eh?" Frederickson remarked. "I hope your rates are commensurate."

"What my rates are don't get my questions answered." Charlie gestured toward the door. "I can ask them, or I can get the cops to ask them. In the end, mine are going to be easier." He hadn't meant to let this guy rankle him that much.

"Well then," Frederickson made a sour face. "I guess you can talk to my lawyers." The he broke the salesman's smile, flashed more white than the average shark, and turned his back.

That Frederickson turned off easily didn't surprise Charlie in the least, but he'd have thought he'd be able to get in at least a few questions. He took out his throwaway and thought of calling Linda – on the spot and within earshot - to check on how much of Trapp Tire stock was held by Gromer Frederickson. He thought differently as he saw Nordella gesture to him from behind Frederickson's in a way that said, "Gromer's an asshole and don't let him get away with anything." Charlie just nodded politely and turned his attention to Liz Wallace.

Since seeing her car in the lot, he had lost track of where she might be. Without giving Frederickson another glance, he strode out into the service area and asked the first technician he saw where she was. "Liz who?" was the response. He explained that Liz Wallace was rumored to be a friend of Danny's and she must be somewhere in the building. "Don't know what she looks like," the tech answered.

That's odd, thought Charlie. Then he saw Liz walking in from a back doorway. She had on the same outfit she'd left his motel with the night before, but she looked just as put together as always. "That's her," he said to the tech while pointing.

"Never saw her before."

"How long have you been working here?"

The tech stood away from the car he was servicing, wiped his hands in a convenient red towel, and thoughtfully said, "Oh, 'bout eight years now."

"And you've never seen her here before."

Suddenly, the tech whistled and yelled, "Hey, guys! Ever see the hot number at the back door before?"

Almost as if choreographed, the techs stood up from their lug nuts and yelled a chorus of "no" and "never" and one "I'd remember that sweet ass."

"See?" the tech said to Charlie. "She ain't been in here."

Charlie saw Liz blush like a schoolgirl, a trait he didn't think she possessed, and then saw her turn around and go back out the back door. He didn't know what was out there, and he didn't have a chance to follow. Almost at that moment – and this is what caught his attention next – salesman Gromer made like a yellow streak out of the sales office and headed for the same back exit. He brushed past Charlie like a bull focused on a red cape, almost, but not quite shouldering Charlie in the process. If he hadn't looked back through the glass into the sales office, Charlie would have tried to join the happy crowd in the alley. But his eyes met Nordella's, and she nodded an invite to him to return to the office.

"Okay, Mrs. Flatwood," he said as he came through the glass door. "What's on your mind.

"Detective, I want to apologize for the way my boys treated you yesterday," she started. They were the only two people in the sales office for the moment. "I know my boys are being over protective, and I have a tendency to take the short view when it comes to them. This business is the only thing Danny had to leave to them, even though my family has money and they will never want."

"I get that," Charlie said, firmly shaking her offered hand. She seemed much more self-assured than she had the afternoon before. "Is that it?"

"Not exactly, Detective. I know that someone has given you the idea that my husband was having an affair out of wedlock, and that I was the one who killed him in some kind of jealous rage." She peered at him as if looking through the top half of a set of bifocals, except that she wasn't wearing any, and then asked, "Am I accurate?"

"Let's just say you're on the suspect list," Charlie parried.

"Detective, if I said I was prepared to reveal what I know about my husband's affair, and possibly about his murderer," she said conspiratorially. "If so, then would you be prepared to assist me in a matter that may require the services of a gentleman trained, as I am sure you are, in weaponry?"

He threw back his shoulders, took a deep breath, and pretended to study the ceiling as he thought. On the one hand, between the useless police file and the interesting – though equally useless – advances of his client, he was getting nowhere. The only thing he was sure of was that the incident with the Hummer was a warning shot. But warning him away from what? From Nordella? On the second hand, he'd expect the murderer to conjure up a diversion. And this information Nordella had could be that diversion. Still, on the third hand, any new fabric in this crazy quilt would be worth investigating thoroughly until he could either confirm it or throw it on the rag pile.

"All right," he finally sighed. "Spill."

"Very colorful, Detective. But I'm not some convict ratting out a buddy from solitary."

Komensky glanced out the window of the sales office toward the back door where both the salesman and his client had been now for some ten minutes. He really wanted to know what they were up to. "Listen, lady," he said roughly. "I don't do interesting conversations over tea and crumpets. If you need my help, then fine. If you've got information, then fine again. But the longer you stretch this out, the more it smells like whatever's out in the dumpster with yesterday's meatloaf."

"Point well taken, Detective. Well, here it is then. My husband was having an affair with this." She gestured like an appliance model at a trade show.

"His job?"

"His life's work, Detective."

"Aw, shit!"

"Before you dismiss me with that paranoid wife look of yours, tell me that your lady friend, if you have one, wouldn't feel the same way if I asked her. Doesn't she think you're married to the work?"

"So you killed him for it?"

Nordella squinted at him and shook her head no, and then said, "No matter how many ways you ask it, Detective, the answer is still no. But I think that conniving wretch of a tire salesman who just ran out back to have a quickie with my rather loose Harding cousin could have."

"Does he have a motive?" Charlie had thought about it when Frederickson had avoided being interviewed.

"He's been hinting at information - information that won't help the business or my family. He's been suggesting it will come out if I don't negotiate a quick sale of the store to Trapp Tire."

Charlie whistled in surprise. "What's he know?"

"That, my Detective friend, is what I'd like you to find out. It may just lead you to the real killer."

His interest aroused, Charlie needed to make an executive decision. This wasn't just a smokescreen. It made sense. Danny owed Gromer Frederickson money, at least seventy-five grand on the books and probably more off. Danny had to have been doing something to pay it off, or to keep the salesman from calling the note. Frederickson knew what "something" that was, and wasn't bashful about blackmailing a grieving widow. But why not just extort money from Nordella? Both the police file and Nordella herself had told Charlie that she wasn't ever going to be hard up for cash. "How high up in Trapp Tire is he?"

This seemed to amuse Nordella. "Better you should ask how high does he have it stuck up. But never mind that. He's the son-in-law of the corporate president Jaime Segundo. Segundo is married to Margaret Trapp. So Jaime married himself into a company that's rightfully hers. Rumor has it that Frederickson and Trapp go way back, so I wouldn't be surprised if she were pulling his strings, if not something else, if you get my not too subtle drift."

"Sounds a little inbred to me," observed Charlie with a leer.

"Oh, you like that sort of thing, Detective? Well, it gets better." Nordella lowered her voice to a whisper. "There have been rumors that Margaret is stepping out on her husband with more than one person."

"How do you hear such rumors?" asked the detective, half sarcastically.

"Don't kid yourself," she shot back. "The tire business is a very, very closed one, and the business end is just as inbred as your leer suggests. Rumors are like flies landing on a dirty breakfast table. They come at random, but they have a definite objective. In the case of Margaret Trapp-Segundo, that objective is jealousy. Now don't you want to hear who else she may be sleeping with?"

"I'm all ears."

"Gromer's wife, her nominal stepdaughter, Mary Segundo Frederickson. Now talk about a rumor." She gave one of those limp-wristed swats at the air that says to the world that you thought you'd heard everything until you heard this one.

"All right," agreed Charlie. "I'll see what I can find out about Frederickson. Starting now." Mumbling a quick thank you, he headed for the back door where he'd seen Frederickson and his client go out, now closer to fifteen minutes ago.

He'd expected one of two things. Either both the saleman and his client would have gone their own ways by now, or he would catch them discussing something about the case, perhaps even conspiring. He had not expected to stumble on them having a quickie in the alley. Unable to find the words, Charlie just shook his head, muttered something about getting a room, and walked back into the store. Was this a random hook-up, or was it meaningful to his investigation? Neither of them seemed to have gone out of their way to cover it up. So why was he the one feeling embarrassed? After all, he could have been out there in the alley a lot sooner, had it not been for Nordella. Was that her intention?

A couple of minutes later, Liz came back through the door without Frederickson. She was not just unembarrassed, but unembarrassed to the point of being crude. "A girl's gotta have a little fun sometimes," she said. "And you got me all revved up and then decided not to pop the clutch."

"Meet me at the pancake house at half past noon," was all he could muster. "We gotta talk." He couldn't get the picture out of his head as he hurried to his rental and got the hell back to his motel.

He got to his room this time without being accosted by anyone in a black Hummer. No messages at the front desk, so he got out his laptop and scouted for a comprehensive list of lodging in the area. He reasoned that Danny and his client, if they were truly eager to keep an affair under wraps, would not be seen at hotels or motels where other business could be transacted. Those hotels that advertised meeting rooms or conference space got taken off the list, and the remainder comprised a list of thirty – including the place he was in now – concentrated around three areas of town: two freeway exits and the old state highway strip. He called Linda, who was cold. But she usually was after he was on a case for longer than she thought it should take. She got him license plate numbers for all the cars registered to Danny or Nordella

Flatwood and Elizabeth Wallace. His client had only the one he had seen, but the Flatwood family had six, which would make it harder but not impossible. As an afterthought, he had Linda check to see if Gromer Frederickson had a black Hummer registered. He didn't.

He checked the front desk in his own fleabag first, but his luck couldn't be that good. Checking all of the other twenty-nine lodging establishments on his list took the rest of the morning, and landed him at a Day's Inn right next door to the pancake house. He noticed that Liz hadn't shown up yet, and came up blank on the innkeeper's registration list as well.

Liz rolled up just as he was about to walk over to the flapjack emporium. Seeing him, she stopped and rolled down her window. "You trading in the ant farm for a roach hotel?" she asked playfully.

Charlie guessed she no longer thought it necessary to maintain any formality after what he had seen. "Just doing my job. Let's go get a table in the corner." This got a sour look from his client.

After they'd been seated and given menus, and then after Charlie had ordered coffee with lots of cream, she broke the awkward silence. Again trying to be playful, she said, "My lunches usually run more to a fruit plate or a couple of dry martinis."

"And my clients usually run more toward the truthful."

This angered Liz. "I usually don't take insults like that from people I employ, but I'll let it slide. I assume you have some news?"

"Questions is more like it. And I don't give a fuck what you take from anyone." He took a long sip of his hot coffee, savoring the aroma and letting the creamy flavor wash over his tongue for a while. He had to cool down before he played his next hand, and decided that it might be a good idea to see just how high the tensions between the two cousins went. He said, "Your prime suspect wants to hire me." Then he waited for the reaction.

It was not what he expected, but that had been happening a lot lately. Liz Wallace just smiled and then glanced back at her menu. Charlie waited, but she said nothing.

"It's my policy to notify any clients when there may be a conflict of interest," he finally said.

The seductive switch went on in her eyes. "Is my ten grand not good enough for you, Mr. Komensky?"

Charlie realized at that moment that she couldn't help herself. He steered the conversation toward Gromer Frederickson by saying, "Nordella Flatwood thinks that your back alley boyfriend may be the murderer."

"That was the first time," she replied.

"In how many tries?" He couldn't help himself, and she'd asked for it.

"Don't be crude. First time ever. He's just some guy I used to see with Danny. I thought I'd pump him for information. Perhaps too literally for you, Detective."

Charlie found that excuse to be as unreasonable as her assertion that she had been having an affair with Danny Flatwood, so he opened the topic. "By the way, Ms. Wallace, I can't seem to find any evidence that you and Danny were an item. Either you covered your tracks well, in which case how did Nordella find out? Or you were never involved." As quickly as her eyes had sparked just a few moments ago, the spark left them, and Liz went uncharacteristically silent. After a few moments, he said, "That was a question."

"I'd like to tell you we were doing it right under Nordella's nose. In her own bed."

"Well, were you?"

Liz shook her head. "There are out-of-town places," she said so quietly that Charlie almost couldn't hear.

So he figured the time for the big question had come, and asked, "Other than you think she murdered her husband, what have you got against Nordella personally?"

The resulting look in her eyes was a plea that asked to be let out of answering. After a few moments, he couldn't stand trying to hold his gaze any more and looked down. Only when he looked away did she answer, "You would have to get to know her better."

"See, now I don't get that. You're doin' her wrong just because of some perceived wrong she'd done you?"

Liz nodded and bit her lower lip. Charlie guessed the water works were about to start, and he reached into his pocket for his wallet. "I'll go pay up," he said, but what he really wanted was to avoid having to witness her crying and feel obligated to comfort her. Too close for comfort, really. As he walked to the cashier, he thought he heard her say something about she had no choice. He didn't have the stomach to push it further.

Chapter Six

The afternoon had gotten hot and sultry, and a breeze blew into town off the Iowa prairies to the south. The breeze had a smell that said "manure" in loud capital letters. For some reason, a breeze off Lake Michigan had never felt as humid to Charlie as this crap-saturated steambath. The additional threat of mosquitoes going after his sweat heightened his discomfort from last night's bites and left him with no taste for staying outdoors for very long, making him gravitate over to the cool air conditioning of the city hall to see if he could shake anything up.

He endured the repeated ritual for getting in to see Sgt. Whittaker, but, when admitted to Whittaker's office, he proffered a handshake that apparently was no longer welcome. Whittaker's scowl framed angry eyes and a snort of disgust. The officer looked away and looked back as if it were a burden to tolerate the sight of him. "What?" he asked in a truly innocent comment.

Whittaker got up and went nose to nose with Charlie, or as nose to nose as they could get, being of distinctly different statures. "I ought to lock you up for leaving the scene and maybe even for DUI if it wasn't too late to draw a blood alcohol test," growled the officer. "Just what makes you think you can dump a motor vehicle in a ditch around here and not file a report?"

Oh, that, Charlie said to himself. It hadn't seemed that important, and maybe it wasn't if this was just a smokescreen. "It occurred to me," he answered. "'Cept it also occurred to me that you wouldn't believe me. Or worse that you'd muck up my investigation."

"Well why didn't you try me?" Whittaker turned around and dropped himself back into his desk chair. "Instead I had to hear about it from a tow driver who thought we already had a report. God damn it, Komensky! I have half a mind to throw these cuffs on you right now."

Charlie held out both wrists in a gesture of *mea culpa*. "I'd be happy to sit here until you send a forensics team out to the location to investigate."

Whittaker looked up at the detective. "Already did," he said. "Looks like somebody in a four-by ran you off the road."

"Got a make on it?"

"Nope. Not unless you can give me a plate."

"Other than the general description of a black Hummer or something that looks an awful lot like one, the only other thing I got is that the driver or one of the occupants was armed with a rifle. Probably a light one like a .22 hunting rifle. Got a lota squirrel around here?"

As Charlie plopped himself into the facing chair, Whittaker said, "Black Hummer." It was a confirmation, not a question. Both men stared at each other for awhile, neither seemed to want to open up any more conversation. Charlie had it fixed in his head that he had meant to bring up the vehicular assault with Whittaker just as soon as he had had the chance, so he didn't feel guilty, and he thought Whittaker should feel guilty for taking so much time going after an obviously bad suspect.

Finally he opened with, "Have you still got that piss ant kid locked up?"

"What? Oh, no, I don't. The kids lawyer got him sprung." The policeman seemed to sag in his chair.

"You don't really think he did it, do you?"

"Aw, hell, no! Not any more. But I was hoping to hold him long enough to develop something else on him. I just don't like that son-of-a-bitch." Then thinking about what had happened to Charlie the evening before, Whittaker asked, "So what do you have that somebody wanted?"

"No more than you have right now," the detective answered. "I just view it different. And I think somebody just doesn't want me to keep digging."

"Your prime suspect?"

"No, Nordella is hardly prime, although she is choice." Charlie chuckled a bit at his joke. "I don't have a prime right now, other than the guy with the gun in the Hummer. I'll bet you dollars to donuts we find that Hummer and we find a killer."

In a surprising gesture of generosity, the police sergeant offered to put out a BOLO, and Charlie didn't refuse. When that task had been completed and Whittaker returned to his office and his chair, Charlie added, "Nordella fingers this tire distributor guy, Gromer Frederickson. Says he's blackmailing her."

Whittaker leaned forward with sudden interest. "Any evidence?" he asked.

"Check with your forensic accountant. Who, by the way, is a very good friend of mine." The policeman winced and Charlie grinned that he had once more gotten under the cop's skin. "But I'm not sure a couple of overdue personal notes add up to murder."

"I'll roust him a bit and let you know what he pukes up." This time Whittaker grinned a friendly grin and offered. "Seems like there's no gettin' rid of you, so you might as well tell me if there's anything else we can do for you?"

Not wanting to waste an offer of cooperation, even if it was going to jump up and bite him later, Charlie asked, "Could we make an official visit to the Medical Examiner?"

Charlie didn't know what he was looking for. So far, it seemed pretty straightforward. Somebody offs Danny Flatwood the tire guy, whom Charlie was starting to think of as The Flat Tire Man, and then, either during the same altercation, or in order to avoid detection, whacks the Tire Monkey Man who works for the Flat Tire Man. Nothing in the way of a personal relationship, or a financial one other than employment, to connect the two corpses. Or, at least, nothing they knew about yet. Thinking about it another way, maybe the whack on the Tire Monkey came first, and the boss discovers it and, then what? Made some kind of sense. So the first thing he asked AME Thomas was whether he could swear that Flat Tire Man died first.

The other thing about the whole scenario that bothered Charlie, as he thought about it, was how the hell close would you want to get to a giant screw whirling in a wrench being wielded by somebody with murder on his mind? If the wrench-wielding maniac were your wife, maybe too close. But otherwise, Charlie imagined, the Tire Wrench Maniac Man would have had to have taken a very vigorous run at Flat Tire Man, who could then be in a position to fend off running Tire Wrench Maniac Man like a matador waving off a charging angry bull. Wouldn't that result in a very deep impact wound? Or if the process had repeated itself, at the very least marks on the body from waving off the charge? So those were the second and third questions he asked of AME Thomas. Just what did the entry wound tell us about the assault?

Then there was Tire Monkey Man. Could the Medical Examiner's office get a sampling of all the kinds of tire irons in use in the area, and maybe at least match the brand to get a better picture of what they were looking at in the way of a murder weapon?

Sgt. Whittaker just stood by and let Charlie run the show with AME Reed. Charlie wished it were otherwise, because he would have liked to have had a chance at the body by himself – while Whittaker was occupied with the AME. But he thought that requesting time alone with the corpse may have been asking too much of this new spirit of cooperation. Maybe later. AME Reed promised both men that he would pull Flat Tire Man out of his drawer later that day and go over him with a fine tooth comb.

On the way out to his rental, in which Charlie had followed Whittaker's wreck to the hospital, Charlie asked, "Have you noticed how much of this case seems to revolve around tires?" He realized how dumb the question sounded the moment he said it.

The sergeant, who had just unlocked his car, turned around and said, "Nothing gets past you."

"No, I mean that different," Charlie covered. "I mean that this case, more than most, the whole community of involved people, with the exception of my client, seems to have some involvement with tires."

"Doesn't seem unusual to me," shrugged Whittaker. "This is a small town. If you ain't selling tires or working somewhere that does, or putting them on, you're probably driving on them or running your tractor on them, or just plain swinging in one hung from the tree in your back yard."

"Yeah, I suppose," agreed Charlie. With a quick wave, he got into the rental Mustang and started it up.

As much as the karmic drift of this investigation was pointing in the direction of tires, Charlie didn't like to take things out of order. He had avoided paying a visit to Danny's pharmacist friend Link Sheffield long enough. As he drove the short distance to the address he had pulled off the Internet, he thought about how he should approach an old friend of the deceased. Flat Tire Man's family hadn't seemed to be too deeply into mourning him, so would Link Sheffield be the same, or the opposite, or something completely different?

Not knowing what he should have expected, he found the exterior of the pharmacy in an older part of Iowa City's business center just different enough from other pharmacies he had known to give him doubts about the owner's sanity.

The building itself was ordinary enough. Built in an Early American, reddish-brown brick style, with a pair of multiple-paned bay widows in front, a centered front door with heavy moldings painted in white, and everything very tight, neat, and squared off, the store could have been located anywhere in middle America. That's where ordinary ended, though, because a giant neon and flashbulb Rx sign in red, yellow and blue, angled from the front of the store down toward the street like Godzilla peering over the Tokyo shops he was about to wreck. He guessed that the sign had probably cost the pharmacist a lot of cash, but less than the neighboring shopkeepers would probably pay him to take it down. Though it was still bright daylight, he could easily imagine that Sheffield's sign lit up the night like a lightning strike on the ocean. He made a mental note to canvass and find out what the neighbors thought of Link Sheffield, then parked the Mustang down the street a ways where he thought he would be when he finished that canvass.

When he pushed the front door open, a little brass bell hung from a clock spring tinkled a warning of his arrival. Before him spread the interior of Sheffield Drugs, which was laid out in three aisles, front to back. OTC pharms occupied shelves on the left, seasonal items the middle, and consumer goods, everything from toys to toasters, the right. At the back, a giant snake-wrapped staff painted above a window signaled the location of the pharmacist. Charlie knew he couldn't pronounce either the name of the Greek doctor who used one snake or the name of the Roman God who used two and wings, but he thought that snakes would have been more appropriate for lawyers rather than healers. Of course, a good pharmacist could overbill a prescription to build up meds for a sleazy legal accident parasite. Maybe they did have snakes in common.

Approaching the window, he saw a young, clean cut man in a white coat. When he cleared his throat for attention, the young man came to the window, but his name tag said Robin Jake.

"Is Mr. Sheffield in?" asked Charlie.

"Today's his day off," responded Jake. "But he just happens to be in the formulary to pick up some notes. May I tell him your name?"

"Charlie Komensky," was all he was willing to provide.

"Okay, I'll be just a minute." The young pharmacist passed into the back room between two standing shelves full of drugs and returned immediately. "Please go through the door on the right. I'll buzz you in."

Charlie did as requested and found himself walking through a narrow hallway that opened up into what Charlie thought of as a laboratory. A big, glass-block window lit the room from the back, and rows of shelved books with titles that sounded like scientific treatises lined the side walls. In the middle stood a large laboratory table with what looked like a movie cliché of beakers, retorts, burning Bunsen burners, and bottles of powders labeled with unpronounceable names covering most of the top. Clamped to the back of the table, a rack of blown glass components with clear liquids inside prevented Charlie from clearly seeing the man he assumed to be Link Sheffield. A distinct odor of manure wafted over everything, and the "kerchuggity" sound of some kind of pump emanated from under one of the bookshelves.

The detective ventured a bit further into the room until he could see Sheffield, who was adding some kind of milky liquid from a long, glass instrument held in one latex-gloved hand to a beaker of some kind of slimy yellow liquid held in the other latex-gloved hand. Sheffield stood about six foot. His body didn't seem to have enough fat on it to make a stain. Although he looked fit enough, his brown eyes had a dark-circled kind of madness in them. No lab coat for this pharmacist, as he wore a tan polo, black slacks and a very elegant looking automatic watch on his right wrist. Charlie couldn't say, in the backlight from the window, whether Sheffield's hair, long and brushed full back, was a sandy blonde or a graying dishwater. In any case, it accentuated the look of madness, as he focused on the drops of liquid.

Concurrently with the intense focus, the pharmacist tightened and loosened his high cheekbone muscles so that they rippled across his thin, skull-like face.

Oh, boy, thought Charlie. I get to meet a mad scientist this afternoon. What freaking next? But he introduced himself politely. "Hello, I'm Charlie Komensky, and I'm looking into the murder of Danny Flatwood. I hear he's a friend of yours."

The pharmacist avoided eye contact and continued with his preparation. "Yes, Mr. Komensky, that he was." He emphasized the last word as if to express how terrible was the breaking of this friendship by death. "And how might I help you?"

Sheffield showed no sign that he wanted to end his laboratory activities to concentrate on the interview, so Charlie asked, "Would you like me to come back another time?" Charlie considered it rhetorical.

"Oh, no, no." responded Sheffield. "I'm sorry, but the responsibility of being the only compounding pharmacy in the region – one that doesn't simply dispense mass-market drugs with all those dastardly side effects – weighs heavily on me." He put down both glass items but didn't remove the gloves. Gesturing around him, he said, "I strive to prevent the demise of the family pharmacy – which is being strangled by the many tentacles of the "waltopus" – and provide my customers and the doctors who prescribe for them a clean, safe alternative to big pharma. My only expectation is that I become as much a friend to the community as Danny had become to me." He held out his right hand for Charlie to shake without taking off the latex glove, and Charlie drew back from it.

"Sorry," said the pharmacist. "I don't know what I was thinking." Instead of just taking off the latex gloves and washing his hands, he surprised Charlie by pulling another latex glove from a large dispenser on the table and putting on a new pair. Once again he extended his right hand, and this time Charlie accepted it and shook it heartily. When Sheffield turned around to walk toward the other end of the table, Charlie rolled his eyes at the idea that he was probably right on about the mad scientist bit.

Charlie followed his suspect to the other end of the table. "What's that smell?" asked Charlie, while wrinkling his nose. "Some kind of chemical?"

Sheffield turned theatrically. "It is just what is smells like."

"Cow manure?"

"Your nose is astute," answered the pharmacist. "As many as five hundred different preparations come from some parts of the cow. I have a number of specimens at my place outside of town, but occasionally there is the need to slaughter one here to, uh, keep things fresh, so to speak. I do it right out on the back lot."

"You a butcher, too?" Charlie's question was half rhetorical and half really wanting to know.

"Come, come, detective," Sheffield dodged. "You didn't come here to talk about me. You wanted to know about Danny Flatwood and our friendship." He gestured to a small desk where two chairs were parked in the corner of the room. "Please sit down, and I'll tell you everything. Did you drive here or is somebody picking you up?"

"That's a strange question."

"Oh, not at all. I was just going to give you a chance to call your ride if you needed more time. I have a long story to tell."

Charlie shrugged. "I have a rental." Then he sat down in the offered chair in his usual casual manner, and kept a wary eye on the pharmacist still wearing his latex gloves. The latter sat down in a worn task chair, shuffled some papers on the desk, picked up a pen and put it into the top drawer. Folding his hands in a manner that seemed odd to Charlie, he turned to the detective and started his story.

The victim and Link Sheffield hadn't grown up together – different sides of the tracks, according to Link. But they had met in college, both in a chemistry class, where they had become good, if not close, friends. Link revealed to Charlie that he never knew his biological father, and had been given up for adoption by his bio-mom when he was old enough to know he was unwanted and sometimes abused. This, he said, stayed with him and colored his self-image until very recently, when he had taken some steps to reconnect with his mother. He didn't reveal her name to Charlie, but he implied that he had always known who she was and where she was.

Of course, Sheffield explained, life hadn't been that bad to him. His adopted parents were pillars of the farming community, and had lavished their only son – Mother Sheffield couldn't bear children – with praise, support, and just barely enough money to get a decent education. His childhood, he surmised, had only made his bond with Danny that much more important to him. It was in his college years that he chose a career helping others rather than dwelling on dark thoughts.

Charlie supposed that Sheffield was telling him he had been suicidal, and asked him if he had stayed friends right up to Danny's murder. The detective was surprised to hear that Danny had met Nordella and quit school to go into business, possibly with money from her family, but more likely with Tim Barside's money, while Link had finished and gone through two years of med school before deciding on a different healing art. Link swore that he had not kept in touch with Danny, despite both of them having businesses in the same, small town, until Danny had come to him a while back with documents Danny had gotten from Tim Barside. It wasn't right after Tim passed on, according to Link, but a "respectable period" later.

"Not only did Danny want my help," said Link. "He wanted my friendship back!"

Charlie sighed. "And the rest is history," he said sarcastically. "So what can you tell me about this formula?"

Feigning surprise that Charlie knew of it, Link went on with his story.

"Tim Barside, it turned out, had also taken a few chemistry courses. He had additionally been put through an orientation course over at Trapp's headquarters. He'd gotten it in his bonnet that he could invent a synthetic rubber formulation that could replace natural rubbers in tires and improve on tire performance. I don't think that Trapp ever let him know what their proprietary formulations were. The course was just so much rah-rah to get the local owners interested in selling tires. But Tim, according to Danny, had taken it to heart, and had come up with at least three promising formulae. It wasn't until I got involved that Danny admitted Tim had acquired the formulae somewhere but had not told Danny where – or how. Just before his death, Tim had also spent way too much of the partnership's money on an independent testing laboratory.

"The formula he brought to me, Danny swore, was a success. He believed this to be true because of the notes left by Tim Barside and found in Tim's safe deposit box. Oh, he didn't start up that way. He sincerely really wanted us to be friends. But after we'd played a little golf, spent some time in my man-cave, and done a few trading deals with stocks –

Danny was good at spotting the investments – one day Danny says to me, 'Link, I think I can trust you with this one. It may help you get the Waltopus off your back.'"

"And that was the successful formula?" Charlie interjected.

"That was all three formulae, Detective Komensky," answered the pharmacist. "There had never been a confirmation that any of the three could be used in a tire and result in any performance or wear improvements. The money for the testing labs had either been diverted by the deceased Mr. Barside or gone into the wrong tests. The tests that were confirmed were lab tests that only showed the material to be non-toxic and environmentally neutral – hardly bad points, but very different from putting the material into a truck tire and driving it a hundred thousand miles."

Charlie shifted in his seat and furrowed his brow. "Where did you come in?" he asked. "This is hardly an engineering test pad. It looks more like Chemistry 101."

"Yes, Mr. Komensky," the pharmacist agreed. "The best I could do was confirm and double-check the formulae and make sure there were ways waiting in the wings to bring it up to some sort of pilot-plant production. So here you had two almost-broke partners and three formulae, one of which a corpse had sworn up and down would be a hit. And we both needed around a quarter of a million dollars to develop a pitch for moving this product to a tire manufacturer."

"Sheez!" observed Charlie. He now saw why there may have been a homicide motive far more compelling than adultery. "With all the tires on the road today, how could the payoff be worth that kind of developmental cost?"

Sheffield scowled and flexed his fingers inside the latex gloves. "Let me give you a brief history of rubber tires, Detective."

Despite Charlie's repeated glances at a big clock on the opposite wall, Sheffield launched into an apparently well-practiced and yet brief explanation of why there would be value in a new formulation for rubber tires. He explained to the detective that most tires still were formulated with compounds made from natural rubber. Chemically speaking, natural rubber was a polymer of isoprene. Many other compounds and materials were added to the tire formulations to get the desired elasticity, tenacity, hardness, and wear performance. These compounds included synthetic polymers of isoprene and of other organic compounds, carbon and sulfur in varying degrees, and steel and aluminum, of all things. Racing tires were glamorous, but the real money was in truck tires. A good truck tire formulation was worth its weight in gold, because truck tires were becoming scarce. Factories producing them were still subject to the vagaries of rubber plants, and too many rubber plantations had been moved to parts of the world where the weather just hadn't been that good.

"Why don't you just start a rubber plantation?" chided the detective.

"I see why you think this is a mundane subject. But believe me, it's a real world problem. When the economy starts to boom again, there could be hell to pay." The pharmacist stood up and started pacing. "I financed some further tests, and I ran some myself. But we still didn't have the money to engineer some test-bed tires and get them into the right environment for testing. Believe me, the pharmacy business is not that good since Big Pharma started playing footsies with the Feds. The only survivors are going to be the big-box stores, and it'll be curtains for guys like me."

"I didn't think Trapp Tire sold truck tires."

Link Sheffield stopped pacing and looked Charlie in the eye. "You see where we wound up," he said. "The independent test beds cost a fortune, so Danny left it up to me to decide which of the three formulae we would test first, hoping we would only have to pay for one. Then we ran up against the manufacturers. Even overseas, nobody had the capacity to set up an experimental tire design that wasn't already in the mainstream. And we didn't want to approach the big global tire companies and have them just rip us off."

Charlie returned the stare and asked, "So who else besides you and Danny and family knew about the formula? I mean really knew about it."

"I'm getting to that." Sheffield started pacing again. "I sold some stock and got to the point where I'd spent about nine grand on lab tests. I felt sure we had the right one. About a month before Danny – you know – we had a big blow up, Danny and me. I'm sure that Sgt. Whittaker must have told you."

He hadn't told Charlie, and there had been nothing in the file. So Charlie drew the mental conclusion that Sheffield was lying. "Shouldn't it have been a blow out?" Charlie quipped. "This being about tires and all."

The pharmacist let the quip run off. "Danny insisted that the only choice we had was to take the primary formula to Trapp Tire. He said he had a connection he could trust. I wanted to wait. I'd had a reasonably good sales month here, and I felt confident I could come up with the extra cash in a couple more good months. Danny said that even if I did, there was no guarantee that a plant and test bed would be available then, and he didn't want to wait until Christmas to get this all worked out."

"So?"

"So I reluctantly agreed."

"And?" Charlie figured the kicker was going to be that they never got to it before Danny kicked it himself.

"I don't know for sure." Sheffield stopped pacing again and leaned both hands on the opposing chair, and then said, "Trapp Tire stock went up 40 points that week and it's still trading up today. That means to me that Trapp let it be known they have a new formulation for truck tires. The rumors were all over the industry before the murder. But Danny never got back to me. He never even called me."

"And now?" Charlie got the feeling that the pharmacist was hurt more by the failure to call than by the breach in the business agreement.

Sheffield turned his back on Charlie and seemed to be looking at one of the bookshelves. "I don't know what to tell you detective. I haven't heard anything since the murder, and I don't have the connections that Danny had. I would hope you would let me know if you hear anything."

Leaning back in his chair, Charlie pondered this request. He now had the equivalent of three clients, or at least of three people who would have him ferret out information and tell them about it. Link Sheffield hadn't offered him money for his services, but he had a formal contract with Liz Wallace and the implication from Danny's wife had been that she had money enough to go around in return for finding her husband's murderer – who she clearly thought might be a rude tire salesman. In his mind, none of the three were prime suspects, but none of the three could be ruled out either. It brought to mind a television plot he had seen some time ago where each of several suspects had had a hand in the murder. It also brought to mind a Christie novel. But he was no Hercule Poirot. Hell, he wasn't even a Barnaby Jones.

"If it helps my case," he finally said. "I don't see any point in making it any clearer than that. If it helps my case you can have the information gratis in return for a promise that you aren't holding anything back."

The pharmacist shook his head in the negative. "Nothing."

Shifting in his chair, Charlie asked, "So who do you like for this? You must have some idea."

Link finally decided to turn around and face Charlie. His eyes looked a little bleary, as though he had been on the verge of tears. "I can't honestly say, although the fact that nobody at Trapp Tire has gotten back to me suggests that somebody there may have concocted a way to get the formula without paying for it. That way, it occurs to me, could have included getting Danny out of the way. He was the heir to Barside's things, and I was nothing. Could this have been a bumping off of a proprietary nature?"

"The phrase is professional hit, and yes, I haven't ruled that out yet."

The pharmacist just stood there and folded his latex-gloved hands, nodded a little to signify agreement, and didn't look Charlie in the eye, but rather off somewhere behind Charlie. Then, suddenly, he took a step forward, held out his right hand to shake Charlie's, and said, "Well, I've got many things to take care of here, so I'll be seeing you soon, Detective. Can you show yourself out?"

Charlie just got up and shook the latex, shivered a little in revulsion at its feel, and made his exit. He shook his head in disbelief as he found his way back out to the street in front of the drugstore. How did he get himself involved with these lunatics? The only sane person he'd met so far in Iowa City, outside of the train crew, had been his old colleague from Chicago. It had been a coincidence he remembered from the plot of an old crime novel. Only he knew he wasn't in one, and he'd been a cop too long not to know that fact often outdid fiction in the coincidence department; and as long as you looked at the right set of facts, little was ever coincidence.

Back on the street, it took him some time to get his bearings. The shadows of the storefronts on his side of the street extended out to what he estimated to be five o'clock, given the time of year, and the cement sidewalk had just gotten back to room temperature from the heat of the day. Traffic, too, looked like rush hour in a small town. After a few minutes, he recalled where he had parked the rental, and walked in the opposite direction to start his canvass.

The first three shops in that direction had already closed up for the evening, and Charlie wasn't particularly interested in the occupants of the flats upstairs; probably mostly college kids renting for the season. He concluded that the canvass of shopkeepers would have to wait, and turned back in the direction of the rental. Passing under the Godzilla Rx sign, he saw that the neon had flashed on and started to warm up in preparation for sunset. "Talk about rolling up the sidewalks," he thought. Who was going to be downtown to see it?

He started the Mustang and thought about how he'd like to get one to replace the Taurus once the insurance money came in, then sat and thought about calling Linda to talk. Just about to punch in her numbers, he noticed a young mother dragging her three-year-old up the sidewalk towards Sheffield's. She had on a tight sweater top and tight designer jeans with an expensive designer bag slung over her left shoulder and held the kid's hand tightly with her right hand. Not an unpleasant looking young lady, Charlie thought, with the exception of the seething rage in her eyes. Without a doubt, she had about had it with her whining son, and as she bent to give him a good tongue lashing, he broke free and ran up to a candy shop window full of plastic chocolates, banging his face against it – as kids do – just hard enough to worry a parent; not really hard enough to bruise.

"Jimmy!" yelled the mother, starting after the child immediately. Just as she did so, a large clump of keys fell from the side pocket of the bag. By the time she got to the boy, put a good grip on his shoulder, and made the boy turn to face her, Charlie was sure she hadn't noticed the keys. As she started to pull the child away, Charlie opened the driver side door of the Mustang and yelled, "Ma'am!" When she didn't hear, he ran around the front of the Mustang and yelled, "Hey, Ma'am! You dropped your keys." He snatched them from the sidewalk in the process. At that moment, his instinct told him something wasn't right, but he ran to her anyway. As she turned toward his approaching outstretched hand with the dangling keys, and then checked her bag to confirm that they were hers, he kept on coming, using all of his weight to pull her and the boy into the next available gangway between two storefronts.

A loud hiss and then a pop came from under the Mustang. Charlie stuck his head out from the gangway and looked back just in time to hear a loud crack, and then to see a powerful explosion rip up into the passenger compartment of the Mustang from underneath. In a fraction of a second, the fireball had ripped up through the floor, blown off both doors, and ripped the unisides from the roof of the vehicle. The passenger door went through the candy shop window with a crash that would have been loud had it not been for the power of the fireball. The driver side door, which he had left open, hurled itself onto the hood of an oncoming car, and the very surprised driver screeched to a stop and scrambled out to safety before his car, too, caught fire.

With the fire now fueled by the Mustang's interior materials as well as by the remaining combustibles in what

Charlie decided had been a fairly large fire bomb, it would be only a matter of time before the flames reached the gas tank. He had started with the rental on a full tank, so there would be a prodigious second explosion in about a minute. With profuse thanks, the young woman and her son took his suggestion that they hasten to a safe spot. He then scanned the area to make sure nobody else was so transfixed by the scene that they failed to protect themselves. Apparently you didn't have to tell an Iowa Stubborn twice that exploding cars were dangerous, so Charlie backed off about thirty feet more and waited for the now screaming fire trucks to emerge from around the near corner.

Probably the most spectacular thing to have occurred in downtown Iowa City in the past decade, the conflagration drew a host of spectators from blocks around for the next hour or so. During this time, a score of Iowa City police, including Arnie Whittaker, had also shown up. When it looked like the fuel fires would burn themselves out without any more explosions, a team of officers started to move among the crowd asking questions and looking for witnesses. Charlie noticed that Whittaker had spent most of his time keeping an environmental team from the state from crossing the established police and fire lines, and wondered how the adept sergeant had drawn such mundane duty. But it was a police lieutenant that Charlie hadn't met yet who asked him to come to the station quietly so he didn't have to put the cuffs on him. Charlie agreed.

After a round of questioning in a small room down the hall from Whittaker's office, Charlie wondered aloud if Whittaker had been taken off the murder investigation.

"No," answered the lieutenant, who had identified himself early in the interrogation as Will Breitling. Charlie sat at a metal table in a metal chair. The only other furniture in the room was a copy of the metal chair. Charlie had seen interrogation rooms like it in every police station in every one of the many suburbs of Chicago. Lt. Breitling didn't use the other chair, however, but chose to stand at the side of the table and lean on the fingers of his right hand. He had repeatedly used the other hand to gesture when asking questions, but it now rested at his side. "Sgt. Whittaker came to me as soon he found out we had asked you to come in for questioning."

"You didn't ask," Charlie pointed out.

Breitling shot him a look that said he wasn't in a hair-splitting mood and said, "In any case, Sgt. Whittaker correctly decided that an assault on a former police officer by unknown foreign or domestic terrorists was not necessarily related to his murder investigation, even though your stated purpose for being here in Iowa City is to investigate the same murder."

"That's how you want to play it?" Charlie stood up as he said the words.

"Sit down, Komensky!" barked Breitling. "Keep your cool and we'll all have a better day."

After sitting and adjusting himself in the chair to make it look as uncomfortable as possible, Charlie gave Lt. Breitling a long look. The lieutenant was noticeably short, but stocky in a way that said power rather than weight. Balding with black, close cropped hair and an annoying patch of missing hair over his right ear, he had a round head and a thin, graying mustache over thin lips that were often pursed as he thought about his next question. In deference to the rather humid summer, he wore a yellow seersucker shirt, open at the neck, with a loosely tied broadcloth tie in a shade of grey that did nothing for the shirt. He had his badge wallet slung over the brown cloth belt of his summer-weight green slacks. Charlie didn't want to look down to see what kind of shoes Breitling was wearing, because he'd then have to break the lock they had on each other's eyes. But Charlie guessed from the lieutenant's appearance that he ran a tight ship only when it suited him, and was pretty loose on the discipline most of the rest of the time.

"Terrorists?" Charlie calmly said without unlocking the stare.

Breitling leaned in, but still maintained the pose. "Look, Komensky. My best man wants to give you the benefit of the doubt. So he's out working his butt off to keep Homeland Security and any other feds out of this. For all the good that's going to do his butt, I expect you to show a little respect and share some information."

"That's just it." Charlie finally broke the stare and looked past Breitling. "I don't know what I have that's worth killing for. But somebody's got to think that I've stumbled on something or that I soon will."

"So what all you got? Maybe I can put it together."

"I doubt it, but here goes." Charlie told him enough about his client to satisfy him without going into his client's tendency to use sex for legal tender. Otherwise, he related the highlights of his conversations with everyone from grieving rich widow Nordella to struggling OCD pharmacist Link Sheffield.

"Yeah," Breitling nodded. He seemed to be agreeing with something Charlie had said about Sheffield. "I would have thought all that farmland would have been enough to keep Link afloat. Family had upwards of five-hundred head of prime dairy at one time."

"I guess that's where he got the notion of getting pharmaceuticals from cows." Charlie shifted in the chair. He felt he had established some kind of connection with this cop, and he didn't want to blow it. "Mind if I ask you a question?" he asked tentatively.

Breitling straightened up and took his hand off the table. "Sure. What?"

"I assume that Arnie Whittaker has been following up on all the alibis."

"Not as fast as I'd like, but yes."

"Do they all stand up?"

Breitling laughed and, for the first time, seemed to relax in Charlie's presence. "Not only do they not stand up. It's just like every other case where there's no evidence and an unlimited supply of suspects. They all don't stand up."

Charlie laughed with him. "I know what you mean," he said. "But do any stand out?"

This time Breitling leaned with both hands on the table – not much of a bend considering his stature. "Komensky, it seems to me you've got all the alibis in that file you took – or, rather, stole. Now you tell me. You're probably getting paid more for this one job than I get in a year."

Blushing a little because he didn't think that Whittaker – let alone Whittaker's boss – knew he had the file, Charlie decided to be open with this cop. "You have everyone either unable to come up with a verifiable alibi, or some people, like Nordella Flatwood and her boys, falling over each other to cover for each other. Like they suspect each other. But I think I've almost ruled out the immediate family. Sheffield would like us to think it's a professional hit, and I'm getting there based on the bombing."

"Well," said the lieutenant, "we've got nothing to follow up on there, if Arnie doesn't get the homeland boys to back off." Then he straightened up again and turned toward the far wall, as if to change the subject. Then he did. "So I'd like you to do me a favor while we wait."

"And that is?"

"Interview Tim Barside's brother, Owen."

Scratching his head, Charlie answered the request. "I was going to get out there tomorrow morning, but now I don't have a car again, and it's getting late."

"No, no, no! You don't understand." Breitling gestured like a baseball umpire calling a runner safe at first. "I'm deputizing you. I want you to interrogate Owen Barside. We've got him here in a holding cell. He was arrested just before we got the call on the bomb."

"I didn't know he was a criminal element."

"He's not usually on our radar, but today it was for attempted robbery. He barged into the tire store this afternoon and demanded money from the cash register. We got him on his way out the door. He thought nobody would call the cops." The other chair screeched out a metal-on-concrete squeal as, for the first time that evening, the lieutenant flopped into it. "Well, what do you say?"

By the time Breitling got Charlie fixed up with a badge to hang over his belt, an attorney had arrived and announced his representation of Owen Barside. A table was slid into the holding cell – Breitling said he didn't want to shit up the interrogation room with lawyer smell – and Barside was seated on the wall bench and shackled one leg to the leg of the table and both wrists to little holes in the side frame of the table. The attorney announced his objection, but gave up when nobody seemed to care. Breitling got Charlie into the cell and left him there with the other two.

While the attorney could have been any of the thousands that Charlie had faced over the years during interrogations, this lawyer set off alarm bells in Charlie that he hadn't felt since he'd mistakenly questioned a Chicago mob attorney in the mid-80s. Maybe it was his three-time-a-day shave, or his two-a-week haircut. Charlie pegged the man as not too many years his junior, and he had the bags under the eyes to show that he carried the burden of defending too many guilty men. Nonetheless, the lawyer had managed to keep his Armani suit pressed and his Gucci shoes shined after a long day in court. The lawyer's brown eyes didn't tell Charlie whether or not he was pleased or pissed to be called from happy hour to defend Barside, and they seemed to avoid contact with the client, as well. Charlie figured him to be fit under the suit, but also thought he, Charlie, would be able to take him in a fair fight. At least the attorney would not have been able to get a weapon into the place. "I'm Jim Wooten, Esquire," the lawyer said in introduction as Charlie sat down opposite both men. "Maybe you've heard of my brother, Big Bill Wooten, the judge."

"Nice to meet you, Jim," said Charlie, shaking the proffered hand. "Komensky. Special Deputy to the ICPD." Charlie never had liked the term Esquire unless it came on the front page of a men's magazine. As a term of respect, this attorney hadn't even earned Mister yet. "I gotta admit that I ain't heard of your brother, but didn't you help this maggot file suit against his dead brother's business partner a while back?"

The suspect, Tim's older brother Owen, seemed to be enjoying Charlie's disrespectful handling of Owen's choice of attorneys. Under the mischievous grin, unwashed face, unkempt hair, and thirty-day beer bloat, Owen probably was a handsome guy who wouldn't have had any problem with the kind of ladies who liked bad boys but not terrible boys. Owen's plaid flannel shirt, open at the collar and missing a button two-down, revealed almost more solid black chest hair than he had on his head. His worn blue denim jeans were just a bit too short, revealing ankles with no socks stuffed into high-tops that he must have bought at the resale shop. The grin said he couldn't contain himself, and he couldn't. "You got an attitude on you, Deputy Dick," he said looking at Wooten and not at Charlie. "But I just call him Little Jimmy."

The attorney took the opportunity to look away and cough into his closed fist.

Charlie addressed Owen and ignored the lawyer. "Do Big Bill and Little Jimmy get results?"

"Haw," Owen laughed and snorted a couple of times. "Only reason he's here is to try to keep me out of jail long enough to work off what I owe him fer fuckin' up the last time. Well, here's news: I ain't gettin' a job until that damn bitch Nordella Harding forks over what's mine!"

Wooten piped up. "I strongly caution you."

"Relax," Charlie warned. "Both of you. We already have enough on you, Barside, to convict you on the strong-arm. So how about you make it easier on yourself and tell me about your relationship with Nordella and Danny Flatwood."

"Deputy!" Wooten rose to his feet and Charlie quickly moved around the side of the table to meet him, nose to nose.

But anything more physical became quickly unnecessary when Owen ordered, "Sit down, Jimmy. If Deputy Dawg here wants an earful about Nordella, he's gonna get it. You only need to sit quiet and post my bail when the time comes. So don't make me call your brother."

It was okay with Charlie. He had a talkative witness on his hands, somebody who wanted to get something off his chest. And even in the whining and bitching that Owen Barside's type usually did about the system and how it persecuted them there were usually little nuggets of truth and little arrows pointing at evidence that hadn't been discovered yet. With the situation diffused, and as much as he wanted to know what Owen Barside had on the brother of a judge and a distinguished member of the bar, he decided to let Owen have his say. "Okay, Barside," he said. "You have the floor."

"Ha!" Owen seemed truly amused. "You say that like to don't think that I ever did any public speaking. In fact, Mister Deputy, this brass mouthpiece's brother and I both went to law school together. 'Cept he passed the bar and I decided to open one after I failed it."

"About Nordella?" Charlie didn't want a discourse on the vices and virtues of a couple of school buddies.

"Nordella wasn't ever a Flatwood." Owen started. "She's a Harding. Always was and always will be. A marriage license doesn't change her spots any more than it did when she hooked up with me during law school. Are you sure you don't want to hear a few tales about the honorable judge Big Billy Wooten?"

At that moment, James Wooten, with a true expression of fear in his eyes, audibly ground his teeth. And Charlie said, "Just stick to Nordella Harding. Are you saying she never really loved Danny?"

"I'm saying she never really loved anyone. She's an ice princess. Cold as the Antarctic wilderness that she was born in. You know the Harding family?"

"Can't say that I do."

"Bicklin and Becky Harding, Princess Antarctica's daddy and mommy, are part of a long-established pioneer family here in eastern Iowa. They have pieces of the action in just about every independent business that was ever opened around here, including that Trapp Tire dump in Des Moines. Bicklin's in his 70's now. So Nordella's never had to beg for anything. It just got handed to her.

"She and me and my brother used to hang out after me and Nordella graduated from City High. So I got to know her.

You know I'm older than my brother by four years, and she was my age, so she was older than Danny Flatwood by about the same. Anyway, both me and Tim got in her pants real regular in those days. Her and his honor got it on a few times, too." Owen pointed at the lawyer to signify that his brother, the judge, hadn't been a saint.

"So you learned that she was cold? Unfeeling?" Charlie asked.

"She was goddamn diabolical! Used sex as a tool and a weapon to get what she wanted, and she didn't care who she hurt. She hurt a lot of guys and did a lot of things and told stories out of school that would make your hair curl. Daddy Bicklin paid a lot of people a lot of money to shut them up. I coulda got her on statutory at the time – Tim was only 15 – so I got some of those payoffs from Daddy Bick. Too late to do it now, but I still figure she owes me for keeping my mouth shut."

Charlie shook his head and said, "There's got to be more. You already got paid on that."

"I got paid some, but Tim, when I told him what happened, kept going back and back and back. And I do mean back. Two three times he and the princess let her old man catch them doing it in some particularly gross way, and then Bick would steam and yell and throw Nordella out and she would say she couldn't help herself and then, a week later, Tim would go back to see Bick with his hat in his hand and tell him how badly used he felt about it and Bick would fork over another roll of C notes as big as your fist. It made my brother comfortably wealthy."

"What was in it for Nordella?" Charlie couldn't help think there was more to the story than he was being told.

"Nordella has always played her old man against everybody else. Like she enjoys having the money but has some secret reason to hate her father. I'm not sure, but I think old Bick is just as hardhearted at Nordella. He cares more about his standing in the business community than he really does about her. Making payoffs for him is just part of doing business."

"So you're putting the arm on Nordella because your brother put his money into the tire business, and now she's got it instead of you?" Charlie already knew the answer.

"That's about the size of it," answered the prisoner. "That and I was hoping to get my hands on some of the money before she had to use it on a defense attorney. That one is cold enough to have stuck around to watch Danny bleed out."

Charlie shifted uneasily in his seat and tried to look stone-faced. Having Owen Barside finger his client's main suspect didn't sit well with him, particularly since he still didn't have enough on Nordella to have the cops go to a judge for a warrant, even with Barside's suspicions. "Okay, I'll buy that you think that Nordella is the devil incarnate. She certainly didn't seem very put out by her husband's untimely demise. But wouldn't you be making the same deal with the devil that your brother made? And what is it about this tire business that is so damned important to you anyway?"

"Maybe just sticking it to Bicklin." Owen shrugged. "I really don't have anything else to say."

At this moment, the attorney seemed to wake from a long slumber and abruptly got up. "That's it! My client's done here," burst James Wooten. "Get someone to take him back to his cell."

Charlie held out a calming hand, "Now just a minute, counselor. I'm not looking at your client for murder, and he admitted trying to get money from Nordella of his own free will." Charlie saw Barside nodding in agreement. "Now that was more of a, shall we call it, a domestic dispute when you consider the 'arrangements' they had in the past. Now wouldn't you say?"

Wooten squinted at Charlie. "You'd be willing to view it that way?"

"I do! I do view it that way." Then Charlie said to Owen, "So, what do you say, Owen, just a few more questions?"

Owen Barside shrugged and nodded again to his attorney, who sat down.

"Okay," said Charlie, leaning back on his chair. "Let me summarize: You don't like Nordella Harding Flatwood. You think she's a bitch and she owes you some amount of money that you have fixed in your mind, but you want me to believe you have no revenge motive when you suggest she was capable of brutally murdering her husband and taking pleasure in the process. You have a law education, so you are familiar with the system and could be cleverly manipulating the other people at this table. And I reluctantly include your attorney in that." When he realized that Wooten was about to speak up, he started talking again to prevent the outburst. "If I get your drift, you also think that Nordella knows more than you do about Bicklin Harding, and that the elder Harding may have been paying off his own daughter, maybe even setting her and her husband Danny Flatwood up in the tire business through his connections with Trapp Tire."

Barside squinted and nodded his head, then he said, "About right so far."

Charlie stood up, and noticed that the attorney was about to do the same. "Okay," he said. "Here's my last question: Did Danny Flatwood know Nordella's history, or did he find out just before he got killed?"

Owen Barside motioned for Charlie to come over, as if he wanted to say something that even his own lawyer couldn't hear. When Charlie obliged the gesture and leaned in, Barside whispered, "If I tell you this, you can't let Bicklin Harding know until you're ready to arrest him. This can't get back to Big Billy, either." This made Charlie glance at the lawyer, who was trying real hard to listen without seeming interested.

"Agreed, and I'll put in a good word for you with Lt. Breitling," whispered Charlie.

"The old coot molested the boy." Barside's face grew pale and serious as he let it sink in. "But I don't have any proof other than what Tim told me."

Charlie left the two men and wandered around in the outer hallway for a while after that. For an innocent-looking husband to find out something like that, whether there was any proof or not, and then confront his wife and threaten to turn Grandpa in to the cops could have been a powerful motive for Nordella Flatwood. Just what Liz Wallace had been trying to tell him. Nordella was no good. To get the evidence was another thing.

Chapter Seven

The next morning seemed like a revelation to Charlie. After bumming a ride back to his motel with a patrol officer, a ride with only one detour for a domestic disturbance on the fringe of the campus, he had realized how strung out he was from a long day of new evidence that he hadn't had the energy or the mental power to process. The interrogation of Owen Barside, followed by a debriefing with Breitling and Arnie Whittaker, had run past midnight, so he didn't feel the least bit guilty about short-changing his client when he decided not to set an alarm and slept until nine thirty. He woke up refreshed, without an alarm ringing, and thinking that some things are better left unsaid. He would have to hold on to what he knew about a powerful local figure like Bicklin Harding until corroborating evidence presented itself. Lord knew that Owen couldn't be stood up in front of a defense attorney and made to look like anything else but a rummy ne'er do well with a taste for the underbelly of life.

After yet another call to the car rental agency, during which he was surprised that they didn't hesitate to rent him another car, he showered and slapped on as much aftershave as he could to brace himself for whatever attempt on his life would occur today. Wearing only a pair of loose jeans and a t-shirt, he decided to spend the rest of the time before the new rental got delivered and call Linda.

She answered her phone with, "When are you going to learn how to use a laptop with a webcam?"

"Dunno, sweetheart. Probably when hell freezes over," he returned the serve. Then he chided, "Then I wouldn't miss your sweet butt as much as I do now."

"If that's all I mean to you, then you're going to be in for some serious physical punishment when you get back."

"Promises, promises." Then he changed the subject. "Hey, did you do any follow-up research on Nordella Flatwood's family?"

"Would you like me to email it over?"

"Given what's been happening around here, I'm not all that sure I'm secure even on this throwaway cell phone, so give me the short version."

Linda sighed, as it had always been clear to her that Charlie would be one of those men who slipped further and further behind the curve where technology was concerned, and she would have to carry him bodily into battle in the cyber-revolution. Charlie almost always had an excuse for her to do the research even if he had the computer screen in front of him. He sensed the next words out of her mouth and beat her to it. "And I promise I'll sign up for a class in how to use a seeing-eye-pad-something-or-other, smart-slab doohickey as soon as this case is over."

"It's not eye, it's the letter I," she corrected, smiling enough that Charlie could tell over the poor cell phone connection. "I can encrypt . . . oh, never mind. You probably won't know how to open the files anyway."

"That's my honey." Charlie knew that an independent woman like Linda was cringing when he said it, but he couldn't help himself.

Linda sighed again and began, "Your prime suspect certainly has plenty of access to money and political power. Her daddy's worth on the high side of eight figures and that's without a decimal point. He donates to all the right causes and supports all the political winners. If you're going to finger her for this one, you better just throw the evidence through the district attorney's transom and be out of town before it hits the floor on the other side. And on the way stop in church in the next town and pray that the DA isn't one of his political cronies."

"That's interesting," Charlie interrupted. "Let's go with that. What non-profit gets the most from old Bick?"

"You sure are getting familiar with the local rabble. But that's okay. I'll delouse you when you get home." This time Charlie cringed. "He spreads the political money pretty evenly, but as far as charities go, he seems to like youth service, halfway houses, that sort of thing."

"That fits with something I've heard recently, but I'll tell you later."

"Okay," she continued without missing a beat. "Insofar as his business investments, he's got more money in shares of Iowa International Enterprises than anything else. But, get this, IIE is the holding company for a number of DesMoines-based businesses, including Trapp Tire. He's upped his holdings in IIE six times over the past year."

He had to ask. "How much?"

"Roughly half."

"Half the company?"

"No, half of his net worth."

Charlie closed the phone call with a request that Linda dig deeper into Link Sheffield's family background. He was still going on the theory that the Indian was collateral damage and the only motivated killer was after Danny Flatwood. The fact that Bicklin Harding liked to support youth charities fit with his being a pervert, but more important was his heavy investment in a tire company whose stock would only go up based on his son-in-law's rubber formula. Insider trading for sure. A house of cards that would surely fall if Harding were exposed as a child molester. Now all he had to do was to place Nordella Harding at the scene of the crime, and that was that. He tried to remember his encounter with the younger Flatwood boy, and thought to himself that the boy didn't seem very emotionally unstable. Just a little overwhelmed by his dad being gone. The elder Flatwood brother was probably the victim, if Owen Barside could be believed. That would explain why Rafe Flatwood was so eager to end the investigation. And the police file said that he was his mother's alibi. But getting Rafe to talk would probably be just as difficult, and perhaps more dangerous, than breaking Bicklin Harding. Once broken, Bicklin could be arrested and put away, but breaking Rafe would leave Harding still out there to take revenge.

The one thing that bothered Charlie about the whole Nordella protecting Bicklin and Rafe protecting Nordella scenario was why Bicklin chose to take cheap potshots at Charlie instead of just having a couple of goons beat the crap out of him in the middle of the night. Bicklin had the power and the political clout to stay out of the spotlight. Charlie decided he needed to know if Rafe Flatwood had access to a Hummer, or any experience with explosives.

Thinking of explosives, he called Sgt. Whittaker and quickly found out that the small plastic device used on the rented Mustang – with accelerant for fire – was of a class of explosives manufactured by an eastern chemical firm and distributed widely to everything from police agencies who wanted to blow up larger explosives to agricultural firms needing to clear land. The chemical company used identifier molecules in its product, and the FBI was working on it.

Charlie decided that he would spend an hour or two going through the police file again. You never knew what would trigger a connection after you had learned so many new and unflattering things about people. Then, if nothing urgent presented itself, he would take the rest of the day off on Liz Wallace's dime and go visit a railroad.

The survey of the police file gave him a few new ideas. For one thing, both Rafe and Danny, Jr., placed Nordella in the house with them when they left for the ballgame – but there had been no trip to the ballpark. These were interviews conducted before Charlie got to Iowa City, and he already knew that Rafe didn't live there with Nordella and was unaccounted for. Danny had not been home. The younger boy had told Charlie he was with the girlfriend, Gloria. Danny – with his faux trip to the library – had wanted to tell Charlie about more than Link Sheffield, he was sure of it. The file also contained a picture of Owen Barside when he was in much better physical shape than what Charlie had seen last night. It also had good photographs of all of the other likely parties, including a well-retouched picture of the President and CEO of Trapp Tire, Margaret Trapp-Segundo. The bio page on which the picture had been printed by the Iowa City

PD had seemed like boilerplate press release kind of stuff when he'd first read it, but in light of the company's connection to three other suspects, he thought he'd read it again.

While he read the copy over, he kept looking back at the picture and wondering what about her seemed familiar to him. The retouch hadn't really been needed, because she appeared to be a stunning brunette, and the photo showed just enough of her figure to make a red-blooded American male want to see more. She'd been the only daughter among five siblings in the family of Walter Trapp, the original president of Trapp Tire. Two of the son's had been killed in the service, one had been appointed as a cabinet-level aide in the second Bush administration, and a fourth was in a jail in London for drug smuggling. The board had elected Margaret when Walter passed after weathering the initial public offering and his daughter's wedding to Jaime Segundo, a Mexican golf pro who had made his money in endorsements. The bio didn't include much information on Jaime, so Charlie made a note to have Linda check him out.

Gromer Frederickson had no particular background other than sales, according to the police file. And Gromer and Margaret were each other's alibi, having been in a "business related" meeting in DesMoines from early that morning. Not enough time for one of them to have offed Danny Flatwood and get all the way to DesMoines.

The police file showed the stock price on the day Charlie had hit town to be over sixty, pretty high for a stock that had been trading in single dollar amounts when the initial public offering had hit the exchange. Loath though he was, Charlie snapped open his laptop and quickly found that the price had gone up another two dollars since.

Charlie made a quick phone call and made an appointment to see Margaret Trapp the next morning at her office in DesMoines. No harm in making sure that the rubber formula was actually real and that there wasn't a motive for taking Danny out of the line for royalties.

Charlie finished dressing in a light green cotton sport shirt and put on his light summer jacket so he could conceal his gun. When the rental car got there, Charlie headed for Mason City. The car company had gotten wise and this time brought him a two-speed Focus with no power windows and no power seats. But the AC worked okay, so Charlie decided to enjoy the trip, stopping in Waterloo for lunch and then on to find his afternoon's passion, the little electric railroad that still hauled freight between Mason City and Clear Lake, Iowa. A remnant of the many so-called Interurban electric railroads that had dotted the country at the turn of the twentieth century, Iowa Traction had been on Charlie's list for many, many years.

As a consequence, Charlie spent the entire afternoon and evening following every inch of the little pike that was close enough to see from a roadway. Twice he encountered an electric freight motor hauling a few cars, the first time tank cars and the second time refrigerated boxcars, and he followed the motor until it pulled too far from the road or into an industrial area that would have been out of bounds in this day of homeland security. When he finally stumbled onto the location of the headquarters of the small railroad, it was already almost seven, and he didn't want to wear out his welcome by asking the people who were working late to give him a tour of the shops. Another day, he thought, as he drove into Clear Lake and started scouting for a good restaurant, preferably a steak house, to have supper. He felt invigorated by the afternoon of train watching, and he had no qualms about spending an hour or two on a good meal and then making the drive back to Iowa City. Besides, the sun was higher in the sky in this part of the central time zone than it was in Chicago at this time of year. Why not enjoy the evening, clear his head, and hope for some idea on how to get evidence to prove Nordella Flatwood's guilt, as his client wanted things to be.

Being from Chicago, a street named South Shore Drive intrigued him, so he turned onto it. As luck would have it, it took him to a modest looking, one story, frame building with a nautical motif. It was sited on the lake side of the drive, so it was possible that diners were given a lake view from the dining room. The raw neon sign above a canvass portico declared it to be a red-meat establishment.

Jimmy's Norwegian Prime Steakhouse.

Finest Dining on Clear Lake

The animated neon arrow directed him to "park across the street." Charlie complied.

The gravel parking lot didn't look at all full, and it was almost half past seven. But fine dining? He was dressed in a sport shirt and jeans, so he decided he'd hang around in the parking lot – in his car, of course – until he could tell whether people were going in dressed in jackets and ties and evening gowns, or just summer casual.

When an old, beat up, maroon Cadillac disgorged six senior citizens, two of whom were males dressed in cargo shorts and polo shirts, Charlie decided he could go in without having to borrow a tie and jacket. Before he could get out of the Focus, however, another Cadillac pulled up next to the portico across the street. Far from being an old 80s model with the remains of a vinyl top sticking to the rust spots on the roof, this one was a black current model luxuriously stretched and appointed with just the right touches of gold and with the initials WT tastefully done in silver scroll on the place where the B post had been widened between the doors. From his vantage point, he could see a driver in a gray uniform, including military-style hat, get out and open the cabin door on the opposite side. Out of it came a striking blonde, not formally attired, who walked quickly toward the entrance to the restaurant. She was dressed in one of the sexiest and revealing casual outfits that Charlie had ever seen on a woman. As he watched the Caddy pull away – not parking in the lot but moving away briskly as if on an errand - he wondered for a moment if Linda could even pull off wearing an outfit like it, then dismissed the thought as disrespectful even for a guy with a fully functional libido.

From the first glimpse, he had seen that the blonde appeared to be in her twenties, with an oval face and lips that weren't made up but looked thick, nonetheless, even at Charlie's distance. Her hair was in a pageboy that bounced as she walked with a model's gait. The beige strapless sundress she wore unadorned with any belts or pins made for an unbroken line from bust to waist that complimented her attractive curves and ended short of her knees. Her summer spike-heeled shoes, in style but still a little radical for Charlie's taste, helped her perfect calves look more beautiful than the rest of her, if that were possible.

Again, as it had with the picture of Margaret Trapp, something about the whole scene kindled a spark of recognition in Charlie's admittedly testosterone addled brain. But somehow, he also knew that he had picked the right place to order a steak. Leaving a suitable time go by before following the blonde, Charlie strolled across the street and pushed his way through the heavy, green doors.

Being from Chicago, Charlie found the inside of Jimmy's Norwegian to his liking. Shunning the typical knotty pine finish he had seen in other country lakeside joints, Jimmy's could have fit right in with any of the better casual establishments owned over the years by the Chicago syndicate. The lighting in the bar, to his right, was just bright enough to encourage group conversation and not so bright as to interfere with watching whatever game was on one of the widescreen TVs permanently tuned to an ESPN channel. The partition separating the bar area from the more dimly lit restaurant had glassless openings screened with hanging plants and railings. The arrangement was sufficient to allow diners to look into the bar to see who was there, but not open enough that the dimmer lighting in the restaurant would not afford diners at open tables some protection from gawking barflies. The dimmer lighting also facilitated a view – through three large windows – of the twinkling lights of lakeside buildings dancing, or just reflecting, off the waters of the modestly sized lake. No boats were moored at the docks that separated the lake from the windows.

Charlie scanned the restaurant area and saw that the blonde had been seated at a table, and not at one of the green leather, high-backed booths that lined two walls farthest from the bar. A handful of late diners – or early, if this were really like a Chicago place – held positions at other tables, and only three of the dozen booths were occupied. He decided that the woodwork was probably some kind of teak, and the wallpaper a dark green, almost blue-green velvet that absorbed light. Some kind of medieval weapon or other hung on the wall over each booth, with the exception of those next to the windows, and lamps that looked like they had been carved from solid tree trunks and hung with rough hemp provided the dim light.

Before being approached by an eager hostess, Charlie gestured that he may like to go into the bar, and he strolled in to see just how much of the blonde's table he could see. He found a two-seat table that afforded just enough surveillance, and let the hostess know that he would like a menu in the bar, please, and start him off with a cold Pabst, thank you.

While he nursed the cold brew and made a long process out of deciding on what menu item he would order, knowing full well it would be steak, he noticed that the blonde, appearing very much unaware of the amount of skin she was showing to the rest of the patrons, drank down two whiskey doubles, neat. When the waitress, a cute but frazzled young woman with three-in-the-morning bags under both eyes and dressed in a blue uniform-shop frock, made a pass, he quickly ordered another Pabst and his steak cooked medium rare. He looked back from the waitress just in time to see the blonde stand up to greet another woman whose back was to him.

"Now this is interesting," he thought. The other woman also had blonde hair, cut barely to the shoulder and curled lightly back. From the back, he could see that she had a great butt and good figure, with long, slender legs in a pair of beige hip-hugging pedal pushers. She wore her sleeveless top bolero style, thereby showing a good bit of healthy, white skin from there to her pant waist. In the dim light, he couldn't see her shoes, but guessed they'd have heels as high has those on the first blonde. Charlie decided in his mind that he'd have to call the first blonde Caddy and the second Tenspeed.

Immediately when Tenspeed approached the table, Caddy greeted her warmly, or what appeared warmly, as Charlie couldn't hear either of them. They both engaged in an embrace which, if Charlie was reading the situation right, became something more than girlfriendly when he saw where Caddy's hands were going under the bolero top. Both women sat down, Tenspeed taking an adjacent rather than cross-table seat, but they continued to hold hands. Though he couldn't see Tenspeed's face, he saw that Caddy's gaze, presumably into Tenspeed's eyes, was romantic, even lustful.

"So, Komensky, it looks like you still like blood on your plate," a familiar voice broke Charlie's concentration. He sensed the man standing like a waiter next to his table, and a full plate landed in front of him. The rare steak had, indeed, bled on the plate, which included a baked potato that looked more like a double-hull floating in a red tide, and maybe a half dozen cut green beans topped with Bernaise that had a reddish tinge to it.

He looked up. "Son of a bitch! Jimmy Castiglia! " he exclaimed. "What the hell are you doing out here in the cornfields?"

Charlie stood up and both men shook hands vigorously. When the pumping stopped, Charlie gestured to Jimmy to sit at his table for a minute. Jimmy was a tall man in his mid-sixties with hazel eyes that could have belonged to a much younger individual. The man still had a full head of think, dark hair with only a few traces of grey on the sides. He wore a pair of black casual slacks and a white, long-sleeved dress shirt, open at the neck. A large emerald set in a white gold ring adorned his left pinky, and Charlie watched as he slipped his lanky frame into the chair opposite and stretched his long legs out into the aisle to reveal that he wore expensive brown loafers with no socks. As if by habit, he gestured to the waiter to bring him a drink.

Curious, Charlie leaned in and said in a hushed voice, "Last time I heard about you, they were going to subpoena you in that corruption investigation."

"Yeah, that they did."

The detective knew that police departments in Chicago and several of its suburbs had reams of paper documenting Jimmy Castiglia's involvement in corruption and in organized crime activities. They had crossed paths on opposite sides more than once, he and Castiglia, but Jimmy had always been a go-to guy for reliable street information when Charlie was on the force. So much so, in fact, that Charlie suspected that Jimmy's actual income came from the federal government as professional informant. "So what happened," Charlie asked.

"I got off easy." The gangster leaned back. "I guess your boys did something right, for a change, and arrested the real bad guy. Not some honest businessman like me."

Charlie recognized sarcasm when he heard it, and Jimmy's broad smile confirmed it. "But this." Charlie's gesture indicated the whole room. "It's a long way from a pasta joint in Broadview."

"I knew some guys that knew some guys that needed an investment." Jimmy spoke the last word to make it clear it was something else. "And voila! Suddenly I'm some kinda Swede."

"I don't think Norwegians are Swedes," Charlie observed, chuckling.

"All I know is it used to be called the Norwegian Castle until I bought it. Just couldn't resist putting my name on it, I guess. So now all the locals think I'm just a big Swede that talks Chicago, and I got a lot of blonde-haired customers, like them dames you seem interested in."

When Charlie glanced at the two women, they were engaged in some heavy conversation, very face to face, almost kissing. He still couldn't see Tenspeed's face. "They regulars?" Charlie asked his gangster friend.

Jimmy shrugged and turned suddenly toward his bartender and yelled, "Hey, Bjorn! Are them lesbians regulars?"

Charlie winced and shushed Jimmy through his teeth. The bartender shook his head. He saw Caddy look around as if she had heard Jimmy's outburst but couldn't tell where it had come from, then went back to her romantic encounter. "'S funny, you know, Jimmy? Finding you out here? I've been in Iowa for less than a week and I run into two people from my home turf right here in the land o' corn."

"Yeah, Charlie? Who's the other one?"

"Remember Doug Christie?"

Jimmy's eyes widened. "You ran into him? Last I heard he tried to knee a hot piece of lead in the groin and it didn't go too well for 'im. Word on the street is the slug had green all over it."

Recognizing Jimmy's reference to the Irish mob, Charlie answered, "No, it was his wife, Aggie. And if that gets back to the mob, I'll know where to come looking."

"Hey!" The mobster held up his hands as if Charlie had the drop on him. "I already knew she was in Iowa City looking into that flat tire murder."

"You still always know something about everything," observed Charlie.

"It's a curse," explained Jimmy. "I always gotta keep my eyes open and my ear to the ground, and one day I'm either gonna step on an ear or kick myself in the eye. Your steak's gettin' cold."

Charlie had, indeed, forgotten the bloody piece of meat on his platter, and decided he would dig in and enjoy it and let Jimmy talk. "So spill," he said as he started carving.

The gangster smiled a broad smile that made his hazel eyes twinkle and showed well-rebuilt white teeth that accented manly dimples and his square jaw. "Even in the corn fields, it costs money for information to travel."

With a particularly large piece of meat poised on his fork, Charlie paused a moment, and then dumped it into his mouth. Between chewing, he pointed out, "You know. . . I'm good . . . for it."

"Just testing," Jimmy tossed off. "I got overhead, ya know. First off, word's out that Bicklin Harding's lookin' for the guy that murdered his son-in-law, and he don't want any of the investigation to rub off on his daughter. So that puts you at a disadvantage, 'cause there're those who would take that in a literal fashion, if you get my drift."

Charlie nodded and took a big swig of Pabst. After a big swallow, he came up for air and asked, "So do you think Bicklin Harding tried to kill me?"

"Naw! Not subtle enough for the likes of him. He'd just have a banker foreclose on your house before you got back home, and when you got there, nobody would know you had ever been. That bomb in the Mustang trick was the work of an amateur. Just plain stupid to get the DHS boys stirred up like that. "

"So who does Bicklin suspect?" Charlie asked this as though he really expected the gangster to know. But Jimmy just nodded towards the dining room where Caddy and Tenspeed were now alternately feeding each other and exchanging some very passionate tongue. Charlie had to turn away from another fork full of dripping beef. When Jimmy didn't say anything else, Charlie said, "That's interesting in a disturbing sort of way."

"That lezzie you followed in here is none other than Margaret Trapp, the one and only from Trapp Tire."

"I thought she was married."

Jimmy just grinned. "Poor bastard."

"And the only picture of her that I've seen, she wasn't a blonde"

Jimmy shrugged. "Take it for what it is, *paisan.*"

Not really wanting to divulge that he had a morning appointment with that very same lesbian, Charlie just commented, "Well, Bicklin's not the only one." And then he asked, "What else do your boys hear?"

"Komensky, when my boys bring me information, they don't just hear. They know!"

Charlie took a leap. "So, was Trapp Tire trying to steal the new truck formula from the now dearly departed?"

"More like there's something else going on about the formula. And that's all I should say." Jimmy looked around as if he suddenly worried that his own establishment was bugged, and Charlie took this as the signal to stop asking so many questions and go do his job. He ate in silence for awhile, and shortly Jimmy got up, nodded a farewell, and walked quietly to an open door behind the bar, where he disappeared.

Charlie finished the steak, left about half the baked potato, and considered giving the middle finger to the green beans. But, all in all, the steak had been worth the price, as most of the food at the older of Jimmy's establishments usually was. Now he had to decide whether to wait until tomorrow's meeting or confront Margaret Trapp, CEO, on private turf when she would be off balance. How would she ever suspect that he would be here and nowhere near Iowa City or Des Moines? If she were keeping a lesbian affair secret, would it be better for her to know or not to know that he knew about it? To make it effective, he would have to at least find out who her lover was.

He wiped his mouth with the heavy, linen napkin and threw it onto the table next to the bloody plate. After he got up, he stepped over to the bar and addressed the bartender, a swarthy fellow who fit the kind of muscle Jimmy used in all his so-called establishments. "Have Jimmy prep my check and have it ready for me up front at the hostess table, will you? I've got some business to take care of." Then, intending full well to go over to speak to Margaret Trapp, he walked to the opening in the partition.

Before he had walked through it, however, the young, blonde lover, Tenspeed, had got up, kissed Trapp on the cheek, and turned to leave. Seeing who she was made him step back into the shadows so fast that he almost tripped on the small threshold and had to catch himself on the doorframe. Despite the subdued lighting, he had a clear view of Tenspeed. He told himself that, for some reason, call it detective's intuition, call it putting two and two together the way he had been trained to do, he should have known. Tenspeed was none other than his supposedly honest, supposedly badly wronged and therefore wrongheaded client, Liz Wallace.

He had been so taken aback by the idea that his client was having an illicit love affair with another possible suspect that Charlie failed to make the attempt to follow her. Instead he sat in the bar for awhile, paid his check, and went outside to sit in his car and wait for the chance to follow the limo that would surely come back for Ms. Trapp. The night had closed in on the lake, along with the sand flies and the other assorted insects and frogs, including a few cicadas that had already set up a thrumming in the cottonwoods and sycamores that rimmed the lake. The restaurant had looked better in daylight, and the lake behind it had become rimmed with twin images of the lights of the other buildings that lined the shore mirrored in the calm water. Judging from the number of them, Clear Lake certainly was more urban than country.

The parking lot was not lit at all, meaning that he would be invisible to Margaret Trapp as long as she stayed on the restaurant side of the road. He settled back and wondered how long she would allow for a discrete exit. He also wondered what this all meant to his case. His main worry was whether the ten grand he had taken from Liz Wallace had come from Trapp tire. That would be a conflict of interest in a big way if it turned out that Nordella was actually the killer. On the other hand, it also looked like this Trapp dame might be paying Liz just to send the investigation off in the wrong direction. Therefore, if Trapp had been trying to silence Danny and it had gotten out of hand, Charlie might get the right evidence but forfeit his fee.

On the third hand, he told himself, almost ready to beat his head against the steering wheel of the tiny and not too – for Charlie – comfortable car, if Bicklin Harding was heavily invested in Trapp Tire, then why would they be paying someone to point the finger at a Harding? That didn't make sense unless Trapp was using her own money.

When the time came, Margaret Trapp-Segundo strolled out the front door of Jimmy's, and, as if on cue, the big Cadillac limo rolled up to sweep her in and carry her off down Lake Shore. Charlie hoped the little Ford would keep up.

But he didn't have to follow for long. Just before the big car would have reached the turn that took it back north along the west side of the lake, it turned right between a clump of trees. As he got closer, he would see that it was the entrance to a bed and breakfast that had a small, dimly lit sign in the trees that identified the place.

The Sanctuary Inn

Bed, Breakfast, and Birds

The nearest lodging to the wildlife sanctuary.

He stopped by the drive and tried to see past the overhanging foliage, but the truth that he wasn't going to see anything without following the Cadillac started to sink in.

It wouldn't do to follow. Even if he had the goods on Margaret Trapp, it would look like he was stalking her. And a bed and breakfast didn't offer the same kind of anonymity as a hotel or motel. Even if they had an opening and he stayed the night, he would most certainly have to identify himself to the other guests, and he just didn't have a well-rehearsed enough alter ego planned for this one. He would have to be happy with tomorrow's meeting.

It was getting too late for him to drive all the way back to Iowa City, as he'd have to get up early to drive to Des Moines anyway, so he decided to drive only into the outskirts of the big city and find a small hotel, even if it meant he would have to pay for the empty room in Iowa City. It was probably all coming out of Trapp money, and, in that case, the less of it there was to give back at the end of it all, the better.

The loud knock on the hotel door woke Charlie from a very nice dream. He immediately couldn't remember what it was about, but knew it was nice by the afterglow it left. He had found a Tourist Lodge motel of the 1960s to 1970s style with the building in a U shape around a central courtyard and pool and gallery type entrances to each room. Taking a second floor room just because of the elevated vantage point and force of habit as a police officer with many, many stakeouts under his belt, he hadn't really thought he would be disturbed. He was certainly far enough out of Iowa City not to expect another attempt on his life, but you never knew. Maybe it was a knock on a neighbor's door, and it would go away. It certainly had been a nice dream.

But the pounding started again. Six bangs by a heavy fist this time. The glowing LED on the cheap alarm clock informed him it was thirty-six minutes past two. What the hell?

"Detective Komensky!" The male voice didn't sound familiar, and the damn door didn't have a peephole.

As silently as possible, he threw on his shirt. Having failed to bring a change of clothes to what was supposed to be a train watching expedition, he had been sleeping in his bluejeans and underwear with no shirt. He found his gun, checked the chamber, and stood behind the door but off to one side. The threshold under the door didn't let through enough light for anyone to see where his feet were, but there was nothing like taking precautions. He called back as authoritatively as possible from inside a small hotel room, "Identify yourself!"

"Wooten!" came back through the door. The voice wasn't recognizable on sound alone.

"Which one?" Charlie only knew of two.

"The smart one," said the voice. It was nasally but not unpleasant. "It's my stupid brother that you met day before yesterday."

That meant a visit from a sitting judge – not something Charlie relished at almost three in the morning. "Who's with you?"

The voice said, "God damn! You sure don't make it easy."

"Depends on what it is," answered Charlie. He stood behind it and pulled the door open inward, gun at the ready.

The man who walked in without hesitation looked nothing like the "stupid brother." Tall and giving new meaning to the word gangly, he had a slight Eastwood slouch wore a pair of slim-fitting jeans, and a white shirt. When he turned, Charlie could see grey eyes in a bit of a squint, again not unlike Eastwood, and a jaw that jutted forward and to one side. Though cut short, his brown hair looked otherwise ungroomed. "Move to the other side of the bed," ordered Charlie as he nudged the door shut with his left shoulder. The room turned immediately almost too dark to see in, but Charlie found the light switch and immediately saw that Wooten had already seated himself on the bottom edge of the bed.

"Put that pea shooter away and set yourself down," said Wooten, extending his right hand in greeting. "We've got some business to talk over."

Charlie secured his gun in his waistband behind him and shook. The man had a firm shake, one of conviction and no compromise. "I'll stand, thanks."

"You always stay this far out of town?"

"Some identification, please." Charlie still didn't want to take any chances. He had not seen any photos of Judge Wooten, and this could be just one of Bicklin Harding's men.

The judge pulled a wallet out of his back pocket and flipped it open to reveal a driver's license and court identification. "Expected nothing less in the way of caution from Charlie Komensky."

"Have we met?"

"Saw your FBI file when I heard you'd been interviewing Owen Barside." The judge put one hand on his knee and looked up with that same squint. "Tough, fair-minded, honest to a fault, and no reason to expect you wouldn't give your investigation a hundred ten percent."

At that point, Charlie chose to answer the judge's first question. "I was out of town on a train-watching expedition and lost track of the time." No reason he should mention Margaret Trapp at this point.

"File said you were something of a foamer," stated Wooten. "Isn't that what they call you train nuts?"

"How'd you find me?"

Wooten shook his head, then looked up again. "If I tell you, can we just get on to business?"

"You can tell me, or you can just get on to business," Charlie answered. "I'm not the one who's been out all night looking for a Berwyn Bohunk."

As the detective leaned his butt on the back of the desk chair opposite the foot of the bed, Wooten began, "Whether you believe it or not, I'm not much different than you, except that I don't have the hands-on police experience. I've sort of come by it in a different way. But I'll tell you one thing. I'm not going to sit by while someone comes into my state to do his job, with good credentials, and let somebody try to stop him from doing it. Let's just say I'm on the conservative side when it comes to law and order."

Charlie gave him a skeptical look. "Okay, you're saying you're on my side."

"Not just on your side, but in agreement with your methods. My brother and his wayward friend Barside would have you believe that I'm just as corrupt as they are. They judge the shoes I walk in by the size of their own feet. I'm betting you think I'm in the pockets of the likes of Bicklin Harding and his ilk. You probably think I've slept with your client, too."

"The thought had occurred to me." Charlie was starting to get interested in what Judge Wooten had to say. It could be big. Or it could be a big smoke screen. He was less worried by what the judge knew about him. With Charlie, there was little to be ashamed of, and what there was had been very well covered up for years.

"Well, I haven't slept with her. I'd sooner sleep with an infestation of roaches. I'd watch that one if I were you."

"I've just recently learned that's probably good advice," agreed Charlie. "But you didn't come all this way just to compliment my skills and profess your purity in all this."

"No, I did not." The judge's face became dead serious and he squinted down at the carpet for a few seconds. Then, without looking up, he said, "If you're going to keep that meeting at Trapp Tire in the morning, I think you should know that there are some serious investigations going on, and I trust you to keep it under your hat unless it becomes germane to the murder. In that case, I trust you to do the right thing." After saying this, he looked up into Charlie's eyes.

The latter didn't flinch, and neither was he surprised. He didn't know what he'd expected to uncover at Trapp Tire, and knowing there was something to uncover wasn't proof that Trapp was implicated in murder. "I appreciate your trust. How much can you tell me?" Charlie knew that whatever the judge told him, it wouldn't be the whole story. Judges are basically lawyers with an all-day ride ticket, and lawyers lie.

Judge Wooten perked up and looked around. "I don't suppose you've got any whiskey in here."

"Didn't have time to get some, and, as you can see, there's no mini-bar."

"I thought all private detectives carried a flask."

"Sorry."

124

"Damn!" The judge swallowed hard as though he had a dry mouth. "Okay, here it is. The first investigation was opened by the State of Iowa when it came to the attention of E.D. – sorry, I forgot you're from Illinois – that's Economic Development. Anyway, they have some regulatory compliance authority and it was as simple as how Trapp disposes of the used tires. They were taking over a bunch of their retail stores, and at the same time they cancelled the company contract with their recycler. This got a few of the owners who thought they weren't being fairly treated in the buyout a little hot under the collar and some calls were made. You and I both know that in any group of people some will take unfavorable changes and turn the other cheek, some will fight the changes but fight them fairly, and others will seek revenge for the changes up to and including just about any dirty trick to get even."

Charlie acknowledged that he saw the same kind of behavior on CPD when there were management shakeups and beat changes.

"I don't even know if the calls were legit," continued the judge. "You know. There may have been absolutely no suspicion without Trapp having used bad judgment and given some bad treatment to both its contractor and its dealers at the same time. But this all got the ball rolling.

"During an audit of the plant in South Des Moines, the state auditor found that it had been customary for Trapp to run a high number of manufacturing defects through the recycler. This, by itself, wasn't particularly disturbing, since it was legal for the manufacturer to pull tires out of a batch when problems were found within the overall process. For a small manufacturer, the proportion of defects or seconds can be pretty high compared to the big boys who are able to spend a lot more money on quality control and make bigger batches.

For example, if you always get ten tires near the beginning or end of a run that are throwaways, then if you only run a hundred tires that's ten percent of your production, as opposed to a much smaller percent in thousand-or-more batches."

"Makes sense. So what did they find? Trapp was just dumping them in a hole somewhere?"

"Worse than that. When they counted the number of tires – and we're talking about everything from passenger cars to big trucks – they found that either Trapp's quality control had suddenly hit the jackpot, or the seconds and defects were just simply missing."

"Black market?"

"That's what everyone thought. So they got the feds involved. FBI and NHTSA. Those tires have gone out there, either exports or domestic. Some might be safe, but a lot of 'em could kill their owners. Too much heat and they're going to fall apart like cheap underwear in a laundromat."

"So who's responsible? And what does it have to do with my investigation?" Charlie couldn't see his client selling tires on the black market, but he could see someone like Gromer Frederickson getting involved.

"The feds are looking into corners that were cut in the compounding. I don't understand the chemistry, but it seems that sulfur is the ingredient in question. The commerce people are now starting to look at whether the tires were exported. But the feds alerted some big users, particularly trucking companies. A few companies have reported pitting in the rubber that seems to be the worst of the bad-compound characteristics. At least a half dozen of the tires were sold out of Flatwood's store. Needless to say, the authorities are doing a detailed job of matching serial numbers and getting to the bottom of it."

Charlie nodded in agreement. "That number work is for people like an old friend of mine, not for me. But the obvious question is, was Danny about to blow the whistle on somebody in Trapp Tire?"

"No pun intended," said Judge Wooten, "but tread lightly over there when you talk to Margaret Trapp. I'm sure she's aware of the investigation. How could she not be? But I don't want to tip our hand before an indictment. So keep your ideas to yourself unless you've got something concrete. Agreed?"

The detective just stood there looking down on this judge who had gone out of his way to not only find him but let him know that motives were in abundance within the corporation known as Trapp Tire. What were the judge's motives? Was he, as he said, acting in the interest of what's right and good and beautiful? Few people were that altruistic. Was he on a mission from his political supporters? As Charlie looked into the grey eyes, he didn't see deception. The man was a drinker, and the eyes showed it. But did his eyes bear the constant burden of trying to remember what had been a lie and where to manipulate the truth? Bicklin Harding may have been a political supporter, but didn't somebody recently tell him that Harding always backed the winners? It didn't necessarily mean that Bicklin automatically made the winners. The judge sensed Charlie's hesitation and got up to leave, pulling a business card from his pocket as he did so.

"Just one more question, your honor, before you go."

"You still haven't answered mine," reminded the judge.

"Oh? Oh, that. Yeah, I won't spill the beans. But you gotta tell me." Charlie paused meaningfully. "Who do you like for the murders?"

The judge paused with his hand on the door knob. "I'm not a criminal court judge. Haven't prosecuted a case for years. So I'm a bit rusty, but I think the Indian kid was collateral damage. If I were you, I'd look hard at whoever interacted most with both Trapp Tire and Danny Flatwood."

Out of habit, Charlie protectively nudged the judge aside, opened the door, and, with his hand on his back just above his gun, checked up and down the gallery walkway. He stepped out, leaned over the railing, and spotted the judge's car and driver parked in front of the hotel office, but no other activity on the premises. "Okay, safe to go, your honor, and thanks!"

The judge nodded and walked swiftly along the walkway to the first set of stairs. Charlie watched the judge turn the corner, and heard the ping, ping, ping of footsteps on the stairs and waited until he heard the judge's driver close two car doors. He leaned over the railing until the limo drove past the corner of the building and out of sight, and then Charlie glanced down at the Ford Focus and wondered when it would be his turn for a limo ride. Turning and going back into the room, he noticed that the cheap motel clock said it was after five, and he decided he'd better clean up and get on

Chapter Eight

The beautiful sunrise that came up during Charlie's drive south to Des Moines annoyed him more than anything else. The drive on Interstate 35 took about two hours, and he got to town just before the rush hour hit. He managed to find Interstate 235 and just barely caught a ramp to 3rd Avenue, which took him south to Barr Road and eventually to the sprawling, warehouse and distributions center with the offices of Trapp Tire in a three-story in front. Next door but down the road about a quarter mile looked like what maybe was or once was an auto assembly plant, but he didn't feel like driving any further after the hundred mile trek that he'd planned for very poorly.

So he parked in the big lot, a lot that had way too many spaces for the number of employees if this was an ordinary day. He checked his watch and confirmed that it was Friday. No reason not to be working a full shift, except for the economy. Not ever having had to do factory work, Charlie forgot how many assembly lines and distribution points had cut back to 4-day weeks in the recession. Then he checked his cell phone and got more annoyed by the text message from Linda. She said that Arnie and the Iowa City Police had wanted him for a two-week update on the murder the afternoon before, and they didn't know where to find him. It reminded Charlie that he had burned almost a week on the case, and the police, too, and no arrests were imminent.

He never did get the hang of using text messaging, so Charlie tried and failed to call Linda. That capped his mood at just under boiling before he decided to get out of the little rental car and stretch his legs. Walking around the empty parking lot for twenty minutes didn't improve his outlook, either. Although there was a switching siding that ran around the back of the building and its neighbors, the nearest main line railroad appeared to be several blocks away. He just didn't feel like getting back in the little car or walking that distance.

The front office building loomed over him a couple of times as he skirted the edges of the lot, and he looked up and wondered which of the windows in the glass, post-modern box belonged to Margaret Trapp. The box looked like an afterthought and seemed incongruous with the concrete tilt-up panel walls of the main one-story building. Afterthought or just plain bad architecture, but he had seen it a hundred times in the sprawling industrial zones of Chicago's suburbs. Buildings that could be thrown up cheaply and serve their industrial purpose, and then could be sacrificed should the land value ever get high enough to make other construction worthwhile. But it wouldn't for a thousand years.

So it was that he walked early into the glass and steel front doors of the glass and steel box that the sign said was:

TRAPP PNEUMATIC TIRE AND RUBBER CORP.
REGIONAL DISTRIBUTION CENTER
INTERNATIONAL CORPORATE HEADQUARTERS
EXECUTIVE OFFICES – THIRD FLOOR
(ELEVATOR 3)

He passed through a short outer vestibule, and as he passed through the inner set of doors immediately noticed the distinct smell of new rubber. As soon as his eyes adjusted to the subdued interior lighting, he could see why. The elevator corridor ran from the front doors to the back of the building, thereby bisecting the rectangular building's first floor and turning it into two squares, and the entire corridor appeared to be finished to look like the inside of a tire casing. The walls had been built out at the bases to represent the narrow part that fit over a vehicle's wheel, and the finish arched overhead in a horseshoe shape. He leaned against the charcoal black wall with its diagonal striations and found that it had not just the look and smell but the feel of rubber. The ceiling was slightly arched front to back to represent the circular nature of the tire in which he was standing – one big mother of a tire. Only the elevator openings on his left and a single information booth on the right broke the sidewalls, while light peeked out from ingeniously hidden holes somewhere near the top of the ceiling, which would be the inside of the giant tire tread. He wondered to himself if there were a giant tire tread in the middle of the second floor, but then he realized that he was walking on one – or perhaps more correctly on a thousand. The floor had been tiled in the treads of various kinds of tires cut into six-inch squares laid down to make a parquet pattern.

At the far end of the hall where, as on the near end, the wall was just flat plaster painted in a silver grey, was a double glass and steel door with stainless lettering above it.

RESEARCH AND DEVELOPMENT

A young man in a brown uniform resembling what Charlie remembered to be a New Mexico State Police uniform sat behind the information booth counter. He didn't appear to be more than eighteen and had a peach-fuzz mustache and widely-separated brown eyes. He had his brown-red hair slicked with something that Charlie thought hadn't been made or sold for at least forty years, and his neck was way too small for his collar. Ron Howard before he lost his hair.

"I have an appointment with your CEO," Charlie said as he walked toward the desk. He noticed that the info-guard was not armed. Not so much as a can of pepper spray.

"You don't have to check in here," answered Opie. "There's another check-in upstairs. Take Elevator 3." He gestured toward the doors on the opposite side.

The smell was starting to get to Charlie. "Is it always this – rubbery?" he asked, thinking the smells came from the laboratory.

"No. Every so oft'n we gotta do this." Opie pulled a large spray can from under the desk and started perfuming the area next to Charlie, who choked appropriately and headed for the elevator, which was parked at the ground floor, before Opie offered him a sarsaparilla.

Other than a print of a race car equipped with Trapp tires affixed to the back wall, the elevator seemed normal: Carpeted floor and wall up to the waist, stainless railing, fake walnut paneling above. He had noticed that there were no floor numbers above the elevator doors in the lobby, but when it came to the interiors, the crazy architect may have been overruled by the elevator company. It made Charlie wondered if the public image for the company were the inside of a tire, what could the foyer of the executive suite look like?

The elevator didn't stop on 2 and delivered him into a foyer that seemed normal, especially compared to the tire guts motif downstairs. But the elevator corridor was only half as long and, as he walked through another set of ubiquitous double stainless glass doors, he saw that the reception desk inside was manned, not by a guard, but by a strikingly beautiful female receptionist wearing a very sexy version of blue racing coveralls cut to a very bosom-revealing V in front and bearing the logo of Trapp tire on each side of the V. The young woman leaned provocatively over the desk – effectively a glass top placed over a row of eight tires – and breathed, "May we be of assistance?"

Charlie noticed that the walls were done in white with stainless moldings. The offices behind the desk all had glass partitions with entry doors that had half-tire door handles. From what he could see though the glass partitions, he was woefully underdressed for this meeting. Far from casual summer office wear, the men all wore business suits and the women wore work wear that ranged from full suits to dresses to copies of the receptionist's coveralls in colors that he guessed to be representative of either rank or department. "I'm early for an appointment with Ms. Trapp."

"Are you Charles Komensky?" asked the receptionist without showing any sign of disdain at his casual appearance.

"Since the 1950s."

Then came the superiority. "Mrs. Trapp-Segundo usually keeps quite a rigorous schedule, Mr. Komensky. You will have to either wait downstairs in the lobby or return at your appointed time." There it was. You're the poorly dressed detective begging for an interview, and we are the cognoscenti. Then a thought occurred to him.

"Mind if I just loiter in your hallway here for a few minutes? That fake rubber smell downstairs really got to me."

The sexy young tire jockey smiled. "Has Barney been overspraying again?" It was just too much. Opie's real name was Barney. He broke into a full grin and gave the young lady a gesture with the back of his hand that said she had his permission to excuse Barney and all of the other tire freaks that worked in the place.

But when he strolled away from the desk, he had something on his mind other than fresh air. As he had been looking back through all of the glass partitions, the thought had occurred to him that he hadn't checked for security cameras. Ordinarily, he wouldn't have had any objection to a security video being made while he was interviewing a suspect, but he would ask different questions and may not bluff as much. He hadn't needed to bluff in this case, but today he would be covering the knowledge he had from Judge Wooten. However, he hadn't noticed security while scanning the partitions, and now, in the hallway, he was pretty sure that video security wasn't a high priority in the office suite. The question was whether it was elsewhere in the building.

Moving out into the foyer, he walked along the perimeter, alternately looking up and down and trying to make the receptionist, who hadn't taken her eyes off him, believe that he was just killing time. There were no pinholes or missing screws in the steel moldings, no air vents positioned high on the walls, and nothing in the elevator equipment that made him think the hall was under surveillance. He checked the minimal furniture consisting of two steel framed chairs and a low coffee table at the front end of the hallway to which he hadn't given any notice as he walked in. He even checked the magazines and small artificial potted plant. No cameras.

Next he would check the elevators. Odd situation: There were three elevators in the building, and Elevator 3 had taken him up to the executive floor as Barney and the front-door sign had directed. Next to Elevator 3 was a single call button, and between the other two was another. When he pressed the other call button, it didn't light. He immediately heard the sexy receptionist's voice. "You have to use number 3." He nodded in her direction and smiled, and walked over two steps and pressed the call button for Elevator 3, which lit up immediately. Apparently the other two elevators were set to stop only on the main and second floors.

When the car arrived with a beep not unlike a Hyundai he had once rented, he strode in and immediately started scanning for a camera. He pressed the floor buttons for both 2 and G, hoping to get some extra time in the car. It wouldn't hurt, he reasoned, if there was a camera and their security knew it, because he then would not do anything that shouldn't be recorded. Scanning for a camera could be considered a normal part of what a detective does. But no, there were no cameras. The ceiling lighting was solid, not a grid, and no fans or other openings. There was a roof hatch, but it was secured by four thumbscrews. No place in the buttons or indicator lights for a camera.

The car didn't stop on 2, the light on the button went off and the car went straight back to the "tire guts" lobby. He walked out and turned immediately to look back at the bank of elevator doors. Elevator 3 closed with a hiss and a light clunk, and Barney said, "That was fast."

"What? Oh, yes, well, I was early," mumbled Charlie. "Hey, do you mind if I just stroll around this lovely foyer while I wait?"

"Suit yourself, I guess."

Charlie wandered over to the doors to R & D and looked through the glass. The area was pretty open and without benefit of glass partitions or tire-shaped door handles. He could only guess what was going on inside, but what he saw seemed in line with general materials research and engineering. Off to one corner of the large room, he could see some heavier looking machinery that he guessed was for prototype testing but didn't really know for sure. A small sign stuck to the glass above the bare door handle warned that he needed a badge from Barney to enter. He could see that somebody had to buzz the lock to let anyone in and out. Perhaps Barney had to take a quick photo of the face of anyone to whom he gave a badge. As if reading Charlie's mind, Barney suddenly said, "We could set you up for a guided tour of R & D next Tuesday." He laughed. "That's the day we have them put away all the trade secrets."

"A tour!" Charlie whirled around as if interested, and started walking back toward the outer doors. What he really wanted was to get the layout of the building fixed in his head, in particular the locations of any stairways between floors. And there was the question of security cameras. If the murder was still unsolved next week, he could decide whether the tour would be useful.

He strode over to the guard's booth and leaned over the counter as far as he could. "Do you have a brochure?" Now he was certain there were no video screens behind or under Barney's desk, but Barney thought he was only looking for brochures.

"Sorry, sir, but we do have a few buy-one-get-one coupons for the local Burger Prince."

"I'll pass. Why don't you just put me down for a tour on Tuesday."

"I'll need your name, sir."

"Bill Wooten." The boy didn't flinch and wrote it down. He had no idea.

Charlie suddenly looked at his watch and, without saying anything further and hoping Barney wouldn't notice, walked across to the call button between Elevator 1 and Elevator 2. It didn't light. "You'll have to use number 3, sir." For this, Barney stayed on his toes. How the devil did anyone get to the second floor?

But he was confident, nonetheless, that security did not extend to video in the elevators, lobby and third floor offices. R & D was still a tossup. So he dutifully pressed the button for Elevator 3 and waited. When the doors slid open, he made it a point to walk all the way to the back of the car, turn to face Barney, and smile brightly at him. He hoped to give the guard the impression that he was nowhere near the elevator controls as it rose to the third floor.

No sooner had the doors closed when Charlie pulled out his Swiss Army knife and extracted two picks that he kept slid into small holes in the plastic handle. They fit perfectly and were never noticed by anyone who saw Charlie use the knife. He quickly dropped the knife onto the carpet and thrust the picks into the keyed switch that turned off the elevator. If he timed it right, he would get it to stop on 2 and Barney/Opie wouldn't know it because there were no number indicators in the lobby or behind the guard's desk. Just when he thought he'd have to explain a second ride from the office suite to the lobby, something clicked and he turned the switch fast to the standby position. It only took him a second to turn the other keyed switch that said doors under it.

The doors opened to reveal that the second floor of the building was completely deserted. Not just deserted, but effectively unused. From the elevator, he could see the entire half of the floor before him, all the way to the windows on what would be the east end of the building. He could see the front windows, and the solid wall that would face the industrial portion of the building. He stepped out of Elevator 3 and turned to his right. The elevator bank occupied the only space on the floor that wasn't just open space. When he turned the corner of the bank, he could see all the way to the west end of the floor – windows again.

As Charlie started to stroll around the empty floor, he looked first for any sign of surveillance cameras. There was none. He started to realize, however, that the floor had probably been recently occupied. Marks in the suspended ceiling tiles suggested leftover dirt from partitions. The carpeting on the floor, a match to the elevators, also showed signs of pattern wear and evidence of recent removal of partitions, maybe even of walls. There hadn't been enough time for dust to build up where they'd been taken out, but whoever had done so had made sure that no traces of the actual people who worked there had been left behind.

He wasn't completely surprised. There were anecdotal stories in any police squad room of businesses that had gone to great lengths to cover up or hide evidence when the shit started to hit the fan. With office space like this – he guessed at maybe 350,000 square feet on this one empty floor – paying hush money to all the laid off employees had to be pretty costly. Or maybe, in this economy, all that had to be done was trade job security for silence. But how could Trapp have been sure that everyone who had worked in this enormous space would want to move?

Once Charlie had made absolutely sure that nothing of evidentiary value had been left behind, he got to the business at hand. It was easy to determine that there was one stairwell behind – immediately to the west – of the bank of three elevators. It was part of the central core of the building that included the bank of elevators, the stairwell, and men's and women's lavatories on each floor. The door opened inward into the stairwell as fire codes would require, and there were no signs to indicate whether the third floor would be accessible. In the corners of the long wall, he saw two other exit signs. Walking to the far west end of the building, he learned that these were not stairwells but fire exits to outside stairs that would not be likely to allow him to get up to the executive suite unnoticed. He checked the east end, just to be sure, but the signs that said an alarm would sound pretty much confirmed it. Nothing to do but try the middle stairwell and hope for two things: First, no security cameras; and second, the best.

Why it hadn't occurred to him that this stairwell would be a well-worn path between the scientists and engineers on the first floor and the executives on the third, he couldn't say. Charlie always used the elevators in his building back home, and he had never even seen the stairwell or thought of it as a way he would like to get from one floor to another. Back with CPD, elevators had been for the infirm, while stairways were open and well marked, except for HQ where everybody used the elevators. Seconds after he entered and started up the stairs, he heard someone enter from the main floor. He dove for the door back to two, but it had locked firmly behind him. It would figure, he told himself, that the stairwell doors to the second floor would also be locked if they locked the elevator. That wasn't smart.

Voices – two men, he judged – and footsteps started up from below. He could be found in the stairwell – not pleasant but possibly manageable – or he could commit to a fast trot up to three and take his chances that any vestibule or hallway attached to the door up there would be unoccupied. He trotted, and he didn't try to cover up his steps. Why would anyone who regularly used the stairwell expect it to be unused by others?

As luck would have it, the third floor door opened onto a short hallway, open on each end. The two restrooms were in the same place on the floor plan as they were on two. He ducked into the men's room and stood quietly behind the door so he could hear as soon as the two men from R & D opened the door and arrived on three. He'd then wait an appropriate amount of time and head back out into the short hall and do what snooping he could before it was time to show up back at the receptionist's desk for his meeting. But no such luck. Almost immediately as he heard the stairwell door pop, he heard the male voices, almost in unison, say, "Morning." Somebody else had walked into the short hall!

He didn't move, prepared to bluff his way out if somebody quickly entered the men's room. Instead he heard the voices of two other individuals, one male and one female, both raised and stressed enough to indicate the continuation of an argument that had probably started in front of co-workers and had been taken into the short hall out of earshot. He got as close to the door as he could without pushing it open, and controlled his breath as much as he could to listen.

"I don't understand why we couldn't have had dinner last night," said the male. Charlie had heard this voice somewhere before. "Your husband isn't going to be back until Tuesday." Aha! An illicit office affair. Now who was it?

"I just wasn't in the mood to have some clandestine meal in a questionable dive and then spend the night." The female of the pair was losing interest in the affair, thought Charlie. He felt a little sorry for the guy, but you get your weenie stuck in the wrong places and you take your chances.

Because there was a long silence, he thought that either the male of the pair had tried to caress the female and she had just walked off, or they both had. But then the man spoke. "I didn't say it had to be like that, Babe. You coulda brought over one of your girlfriends." Charlie immediately recognized the male voice as that of Gromer Frederickson and concluded the female had to be Margaret Trapp. Then he marveled at what he'd just heard. One of her girlfriends? One?

"You couldn't keep up." She was teasing.

"Try me."

"You're not getting any until you've cleaned up this mess with Danny Flatwood." Charlie couldn't believe his luck. She had virtually accused Frederickson of murder!

"The securities boys and most of our stockholders still think it's a go on Danny's formula. I've made sure it grinds in the rumor mill to a fine powder. If we can hold it there until we sell the remaining subordinated bonds, it won't matter if we tell the world it's a flop."

"Okay, maybe you've earned one girlfriend." Her voice had suddenly gotten playful. Charlie wasn't so sure any more that the mess with Danny meant murder or just lies about the formula – the formula that Link Sheffield was hanging his financial future on. "Did you pay off the pharmacist?" Speak of the devil.

"He's a loose cannon," said the male voice – Frederickson – this time. When I finally decided we'd have to tell him that the formula tested badly, he went bonkers. I offered to pay him whatever he wanted to keep his mouth shut for awhile, and he just said he'd get his payback from the people that were trying to ruin him. I didn't know what that meant, so I let it rest." So, thought Charlie, Link had lied to him.

"Idiot!" she yelled loud enough that Charlie jumped away from the door. "Take care of that asshole now. We can't have him going to the markets with what he knows." Charlie wished he had a recorder, but he didn't. Chalk it up to trying to roll a train-watching trip into business.

"Listen, Doll. I've cleaned up enough of your messes that you can cut me a little slack. You wouldn't want that lazy rich bastard of a golfing husband of yours to find out about our little sex parties, would you?"

There was a pause, and Charlie couldn't tell if that was because Margaret was angry at Frederickson or just because she was building up steam. "Don't forget where the money comes from," she finally ordered. Her voice sounded angry and threatening. "If you cut me off, then you cut yourself off. And I'll have one of my bondage girlfriends find you and cut something else off, too. Besides," she huffed. "You won't do it. There's no money in it for you to out me to dear, sweet Jaimito. So take all that misplaced testosterone and get something right for a change."

"I made this company." It was a proud declaration.

"And there's not enough money left in it to satisfy all the creditors right now, so keep it in mind when you start that insufferable male bragging of yours."

He heard what sounded like a scuffle, and Charlie was tempted to make sure that Frederickson wasn't strangling his boss. He took the chance and cracked to door just enough to see that, contrary to what he thought, they were passionately embracing. It wouldn't be easy to divide and conquer these two.

They separated wordlessly. Charlie assumed that she was going back to her office for their scheduled meeting and Frederickson was going to find a way to silence Link Sheffield. It was time to find his way back downstairs and make a more respectable entry to the third floor. It wasn't until that moment that he remembered what he had forgotten. He had left the only operating elevator stuck on the second floor.

Barney had perp-walked him into Margaret Trapp's office with his hands behind his back and secured by a plastic cable tie. The hayseed guard hadn't even looked for Charlie's gun, which still rested inside his jacket, and hadn't been given any resistance. Charlie had always thought when you put yourself in a spot because you forgot to do something, it was for a reason. Maybe he now had the advantage of having Ms. Trapp doubt her superiority and wonder just exactly how much he knew or had found out.

Standing there at her desk, she looked like her picture now. He could see the resemblance to the woman who had trysted with her lover at Jimmy's, but the woman before him more closely matched the young, though much more conservative, look of her publicity shots. Amazing what an expensive blonde wig can do. He felt Barney's gun at the back of his neck and bristled a little. It worried him the way Barney was holding it. If it went off, it would be an accident, not intentional. "Hey, Kid! When this is over, let me take you out to the range and show you some pointers so you don't kill somebody with that pea shooter unless you mean it."

Still holding the gun with the muzzle at the base of his skull, Barney reached around, pulled Charlie's wallet out of his jacket, and tossed it onto the desk in front of Margaret. She opened it and found his drivers license first. "Charlie Komensky, my morning appointment. I guess I should have expected a private dick to be dicking around." She put the card back into its pocket and didn't go any further, but looked up into his eyes. He noticed hers were clear and intense, driven even. "Well?"

"I had some time to kill and got curious about your second floor. It's your fault for being so damned punctual." He hoped that she would assume he had only gotten to the second floor.

She chuckled and said, "Yes. They told me you got here a bit early." Then to Barney, "I think Mr. Komensky is benign, if not completely harmless. Cut that thing off and let him sit down. We have a meeting scheduled."

"You're too gracious," he said, sitting down across the desk from her as soon as the guard obliged. As Barney got to the door, he couldn't resist another dig. "The offer to teach you how to shoot still stands, buddy."

She sat, too, and looked across the desk at him. A chill ran through him. The raw sexual power of this woman suddenly made him understand why so many seemed to lust for her, and told him that she wouldn't have hesitated to have Barney pull the trigger if she had wanted to. "It's your meeting, Mr. Komensky," she opened.

"Lady, you know why I'm here." He got it out flat so that it was clear he didn't doubt what he was saying. But she was unruffled.

"I understand you're investigating the unfortunate death of one of the dealers." He saw it as significant that she didn't say "our dealers." She didn't want to own any responsibility.

"Where were you on the morning of the murder?"

"I think we established with the police that we were here in an early breakfast meeting." I think. I understand. He could see she was a political animal. Then she added, "Where were you?"

"Safe in a stack of pancakes and side of bacon at an I-Hop in Melrose Park, and blissfully ignorant of anything related to your magnificent tire company."

She stood up as if to expound on the subject and started walking around the desk. "The tire business isn't so bad, Mr. Komensky. It has been in my family ever since pneumatic tires and gas-engine road vehicles became a primary means of transportation." He started to notice her dress, which was just a little too night-clubby for the morning and the office. Very snug, with clean lines in an off white cotton blend, it flattered her figure and showed ample cleavage. She continued to walk until she was behind him, but he didn't turn around. "I gather you think someone here at Trapp Tire had something to do with it."

"I think Danny threatened to go public with truth instead of rumor about his truck tire compounding and somebody silenced him to keep your stock price up."

Her left hand suddenly rested on his shoulder and moved lightly down the front of his jacket. "Interesting," she said. Her hand stopped where she could feel the bulk of his gun in its shoulder holster. "I like that."

Her attempt at seduction wasn't unlike Liz Wallace at the motel room, except he didn't expect Margaret Trapp to disrobe in the open environment of the office suite. He ignored the gambit. "I think your Mr. Gromer Frederickson may have had something to do with it."

She laughed a hearty but slightly evil laugh and withdrew her hand. As she continued her walk full circle back to her desk chair, he noticed she was wearing four-inch heels and they did an excellent job of emphasizing her positive. She stopped and stood behind her chair. "If only Gromer actually had big enough stones to do something like that." She sighed. "Unfortunately, Mr. Komensky, or may I call you Charlie?" He nodded. "Unfortunately, Charlie, his methods consist entirely of spending far too much of my money to get people to do far too little of what I would like them to do."

"And what if he gets desperate?"

"Desperation comes in a lot of different flavors, Charlie. For example, you must have been pretty desperate to be snooping around doing what some of us might call corporate espionage." She pulled open her top desk drawer. "Are you desperate enough to shoot me?"

"Only if you pull a gun out of that drawer and point it in my direction."

Instead she withdrew a single sheet of paper on which had been printed a digital photo. She dropped it onto her desktop so that it slid towards Charlie. The color picture didn't do Liz Wallace justice, showing her standing naked in front of him in his hotel room. "Has the flavor of your desperation changed any?"

As bad as it would look for him to be cavorting with a female client – and that was not what the photograph showed – he worried more that he had been played by his client yet again. If Liz Wallace was so interested in pointing suspicion at Danny's wife, why would she sabotage the investigation of the real killer by giving this photo to her gay lover? Unless even Liz was now starting to think that the CEO of Trapp Tire really did have something to do with it. "If this is a blackmail attempt, I'll save you the trouble. You can send that right off to the Illinois State Police, and I'm sure you know the email address for Sgt. Whittaker." He pushed the piece of paper back to her and stood up. "And now, if you don't mind, I think our little meeting is over, and I'm going to call Sgt. Whittaker and have him put a detail on Link Sheffield."

The color drained from Margaret Trapp's face. It had suddenly dawned on her that he knew more than she wanted him to. "Wait, detective. Charlie!"

He paused. "You just told me that Gromer Frederickson could actually be more desperate than you let on." As much as he wanted to ask her about her relationship to his client, he decided that figurative card was an ace in the hole for another deal, and he turned and left.

Chapter Nine

As soon as he got into his rented car, Charlie called Arnie Whittaker. He hadn't put all the pieces together, like where the murder weapon was, or even what it was. But he didn't want the death of Link Sheffield on his conscience. It still gnawed at him why Frederickson as number one suspect wouldn't have tried to stop him from meeting with Margaret. She must have told him who she was meeting with, and Frederickson certainly had spared no past effort – if he was the killer – in getting Charlie out of the way. Aggressive interventions like assault with a motor vehicle and attempted murder by explosive don't usually get followed by standing around and waiting to see what happens.

The drive east on Interstate 80 was pleasant enough. He found a local country station on the radio, choosing to eschew the impersonal country stations he could get on the rental's functional satellite radio, and let his mind pick through the clutter of what he knew and didn't know about the murders of Danny Flatwood and his employee, Seth Sharedream. But, despite the fact that he had warned Sgt. Whittaker, he couldn't escape the need to push the little car up to 80 and 85 on the stretches with moderate traffic.

First, he thought about his client. He now realized that Margaret Trapp had put his client up to planting a camera and taking the picture in his motel room. Maybe it had only been for future insurance in case he caught on to the fact that Danny and Link Sheffield's tire formula wasn't the saving grace of Trapp Tire. Maybe Liz had seen it as a way to keep him focused on Nordella Flatwood. Either way, just about anything she said couldn't be trusted. The thought also crossed his mind that Nordella could also have been one of Margaret's girlfriends, but he dismissed that as unfounded. What was Liz Wallace's alibi again? Oh, yeah, she had been at the nail salon first thing that morning because she had broken an extension the night before. Convenient, and the alibi had been checked, but the nail girl could probably be bribed.

So, as the corn and alfalfa drifted by, his mind wandered over to Nordella. At least one of her kids thought she had done it. He wondered why, because the motive of finding out that Danny was stepping out was a slim one. And Nordella, being a Harding, didn't have anything else but revenge to gain by killing Danny. Offing Danny with a giant bolt to the brain was hardly revenge served cold. Her alibi had Nordella at home the morning of the murders, and Charlie just couldn't see why she couldn't bribe somebody to cover that one. The Flatwood brothers didn't seem to like each other enough to perjure themselves for each other.

Moving on to Owen Barside. Was there something else about Nordella that he hadn't told Charlie? Something that the older Flatwood brother had found out about? And that was why they didn't want Charlie snooping too deeply into Nordella's past and present? Charlie believed Owen when he said he didn't kill Danny, no matter how thin his alibi or thick his motive.

Link Sheffield didn't, at first glance, seem capable of murder. Charlie thought of pharmacy as something you did when you wanted to be a doctor but didn't have the guts – pun intended – to cut something open. When had Gromer Frederickson said he had told Link about the failure of the tests on his new rubber formula? He probably hadn't. Charlie couldn't remember exactly and that bothered him. Had the pharmacist actually told Charlie straight out that he didn't know of the outcome of the tests? You bet he had. Okay, alibi. Oh, yes. He was on a buying trip to Des Moines that morning. He had the parking garage chits to show for it, and they put him out of town at time of death. Had they checked for security video at the parking garage? For correct timing on the machine that issued the chits? Stick out your chit and say aha!

He was just about to start looking for a pull-off or get ready to take the next exit when his cell phone rang. Charlie didn't usually answer the phone when he was driving. He wasn't concerned about safety, as such, but that he'd accidentally press the wrong button and lose the call. Better to let somebody leave a message. And he hated those damn blue things. Whenever somebody wore one during a meeting with him, he just wanted to rip it off the person's head, and the ear along with it. He grabbed it and asked the caller for a second to pull off. The next exit took him up an embankment and onto the state road, which he crossed after rolling the stop sign. He pulled to a stop on a wide gravel shoulder for the corresponding entrance ramp where truckers had obviously been doing the same for years.

He looked at the call ID, then said into the flip phone, "I was just going to call you."

Arnie Whittaker's voice urgently asked, "Where are you?"

He looked around for a sign, but couldn't see any. "Some state road entrance ramp with lots of truck traffic. Why?"

"Seen anything unusual?"

"Don't think so."

"Then you'll find out in a few miles. When you get there, stay put. Ask for the state cop in charge. I'm on my way out." The line released before Charlie could say WTF.

It took him about three minutes to get a drink of water from a bottle he'd bought at Casey's on the way out of town, to get back on the road, and to get up to speed. As he got up over the next rise east, he could see the police cruisers "advertising" about three miles ahead. Must've been a one helluva crash!

Three and a half minutes later, he was on the ground asking troopers where to find the incident commander. He had parked beyond the accident and had started walking back to it. He could see that the accident had apparently involved a powder blue IS250 with a sunroof and satellite radio and what appeared to be Illinois plates. The next Iowa State Trooper he encountered, he showed his ICPD badge and asked what had happened.

"Near as I can tell it's a one-car, one-bag accident. But you'll have to ask the lieutenant there around the other side."

As Charlie continued walking back – he had drifted a good quarter mile past the actual wreck – he started to see that there was not a piece of metal or trim on the car that hadn't been distorted by the crash impact somehow. The vehicle rested on its right side with the nose pointed to the west. The trunk and the hood had both popped open. Steam rose from the engine, and he could see that, before coming to rest, the vehicle had just missed going into the meander of a small but rushing creek that came close to the south side of the right of way. Charlie shivered. This was what the black Hummer had tried to do to him. A metal guard rail had become completely involved with the car, with part of it lodged in the rear suspension and another part protruding from the backlight. He looked around – mostly from reflex – just to see if there was a black SUV hovering somewhere on the horizon with its driver watching the deadly results of his or her actions.

The body, now draped in an orange piece of canvas from the back of one of the patrol cars, had probably been ejected and thrown a good fifty feet. Charlie had been to a hundred drunk-driving accidents like this, where the driver had suddenly found himself drifting, then over corrected and wound up running off the road sideways. If there were enough momentum, the vehicle would almost always flip or roll or both. This had been both, and Charlie could judge the spot where the vehicle went off from the skid marks. The body was far to the south of that trajectory. In tall grass that had been trampled by the first responders, it, too, had just missed going into the drink. But what was the significance of this accident, and why did Whittaker want him here?

He turned again and noted the Illinois vanity plate:

GHF GOLD

What was the significance of that?

"Lieutenant," he called when close enough. "Charlie Komensky. Sgt. Whittaker from Iowa City said to speak to you."

The young lieutenant, who looked more like a body-builder in a uniform than a typical desk jockey supervisor type – fat and lazy – looked up from his notes and smiled a warm smile. "Grace. Trooper Lt. Grace, Sir." He held out a welcoming hand. "Whittaker said you'd want to be in on this. You ready?" He gestured for Charlie to walk to the corpse.

"Got an ID?"

"Forty year old male, Gromer Frederickson, white, single, out of Des Moines. You know him?" Charlie was connecting the license plate and wondering what the H stood for when the trooper said. "Middle name Hortens. Can you imagine anyone's mother naming him that?"

"I would have guessed Hitman. Yeah, I've met him and then some."

The lieutenant pulled up the corner of the cover closest to them both. Although Charlie had seen many corpses in his career, he was never ready for the sheer ugliness of a head torn apart by a high powered round. "Again, pending the ME, the best we can say is he took a round into the left temple from somewhere north, but until we find the round that did this and get the ME, range is unknown. It's also hard to tell how far the car may have traveled on cruise before rolling. Could be a quarter to a half mile if the suspension was in good alignment. The road is in good shape, and these babies – he gestured at the car – don't creep or hunt much if they're maintained right."

"Big mystery, huh?" Charlie was already thinking that this blew his whole theory of Frederickson being Danny's murderer, although . . . "What time was this called in?"

"Just a little after ten."

Almost certainly happened before he had left the parking lot at Trapp Tire. Really too little time for Margaret Trapp to decide that her golden boy was a liability, give the word to a henchman, any henchman, and get set up for what had to be a difficult shot, even for a top marksman. Frederickson had pretty much hit the road after his *tete a tete* with Margaret and blew right into this trouble. "Mind if I look around?"

"I don't think there's much damage you can do. Want a pair of gloves?"

Charlie took the latex gloves from the lieutenant and stuffed them into his pocket. After making a wide circle of the car, noting everything, he concluded that, Frederickson would have been a goner whether he survived the gunshot wound or not. Until the car was turned upright, and that would be after forensics said it was okay, he wouldn't be able to check the contents of the interior. What he could do was take a good look at the trunk. He was prepared to note any contents but there weren't any. No briefcase or laptop computer, no box of papers stashed in a corner. If they had been there, they had been thrown out along with the driver as the car pinwheeled to its current position.

Putting a glove on his right hand, he reached in and gingerly lifted the cover over the spare tire. He found it intact, along with the jack and tire iron, but only because it had been properly secured. Nothing else in the tire well.

As he stood up, he saw the Iowa City cop car careening west with siren going and warning lights ablaze. It slowed suddenly, and its driver caught the next crossover of the median west, kicking up dust and rocks, and maneuvered it into the already squeezed eastbound traffic until it was abreast of Charlie. Before it came to a stop, Sgt. Arnie Whittaker had the door open. He made a half running, half walking exit and jogged over to where Charlie stood amazed at the spectacle. "You should sell that bit to the movies," Charlie observed.

"Figured I had to get here before you hurt yourself," was the reply. "You can take out an eye with one of those gloves."

"Yeah, they make great condoms, too, if you're from a hick PD that has five dicks." The two men finally acknowledged each other and each grinned and shook hands.

Then Whittaker turned to look at the wreck. "You hear 'em on the radio, but you're never really ready for what you're gonna see. Where's the body?"

"Over there. Looks like an expert shooter spilled his bucket before he even knew what hit him."

Whittaker shook his head. "I've got permission from the capital to bring AME Thomas out from IC. He should be only a few minutes behind me."

"That's all well and good. But unless we get lucky and the slug's in the car, it's going to be a long night combing the grass back there." Charlie pointed back over the road. "Got any other good news?"

"When I heard it was Frederickson," started Whittaker.

"Yeah," Charlie interrupted. "I was wondering why a high seller for a Des Moines company has Illinois plates."

"Don't get ahead of me. We ran the plates and found out that Frederickson's got a home he maintains in – where was it?" He hesitated and pulled a notepad out of his back pocket. Thumbing the pages, he banged the right one with his forefinger when he found it. "Bureau, Illinois. It's what you Illinoisians call a 'farmette.'"

"Well, all I know is that a farmette is something you get when you divide up farmland to build middle class houses. But I had reason to think that Frederickson was going to put the pharmacist's life in danger, and here we have him the victim of an all too obvious hit. I think we need to find out what's out there."

Whittaker laughed. "Ahead of you again. West Central Illinois FBI is on their way over there with a probably cause warrant right now. Hope you're right about him and Trapp using criminal coercion to manipulate the stock price. I'd look pretty silly."

Just then, they noticed one of the uniformed troopers who had been beating the high grass west of them walking toward them with something in a large and heavy in a white plastic bag. When they acknowledge him, he said, "Boss says you'll want to see this. Sorry for the non-standard bag, but we ran out."

Whittaker gloved both hands, reached into the bag and pulled out a tire iron. Both of them looked at the trooper with open mouths, and then Charlie asked, "Where'd this come from?"

"Fifteen feet west northwest of the body. It was on top of some grass that was still green underneath it, so it probably came out of the car. We got a bunch of pictures. Boss thinks that's a blood stain."

Looking at the curved end with the nut wrench, both of them could see the brownish stain, and both agreed. They could finally have the murder weapon. But if Gromer wasn't the murderer, what was he doing with it? They were still looking at the wrench when the ME's van pulled up. The driver had apparently gone all the way to the next exit to make the turn around rather than making the Dukes of Hazard display made by Whittaker.

AME Thomas got out and strode toward them. "Whatcha got there, boys?"

"We were thinking you'd need a tire change after wearing off all that extra rubber going down to 48 to make a turn." Arnie thrust the tire iron out at Thomas' face so the latter had to stumble back a step to focus on it. "That blood?"

"Ninety percent sure it is. Who's the vic?"

Charlie piped up. "With any luck, Seth Sharedream. Can you expedite the blood match and also check for any trace DNA for the perp?" Thomas gave the iron and bag to his tech and told him to drive it back to IC non-stop, then come back to the scene.

"Looks like we'll be here for awhile," Thomas observed when he was done with the tech.

All three had started walking toward Frederickson's body when Charlie stopped short. "If Frederickson did the flat tire murders, why did he keep the tire iron?"

Whittaker and the AME stopped with him, and the cop faced him. "I don't know. What if it's not even Sharedream's blood?"

"What if it is?"

"Then he was stupid."

"No. No. Follow me on this. If he was the murderer, he would have disposed of the murder weapon. There's a thousand miles of river along here that he could have thrown it into, and it would have been harder and harder to get a DNA match the longer it was under water. But he had it in his trunk. And he wouldn't be laying here with his brains sprayed over half the past quarter mile if he was just a murderer. But maybe he's a blackmailer."

The AME chimed in. "You think he got it from somebody and he was holding it over them?"

Giving Thomas tacit agreement, Charlie turned to Whittaker. "Do the news shops have this one yet?"

"As far as they are concerned, this is just another drunk going off the road and killing himself without further ado. The only way were going to have news vans way out here is if one of the stringers accidentally drives by. Why? What's your idea?"

"Can you get your people to round up my client and Margaret Trapp and bring them out here to the scene? And do it before we move the body?"

"We can ask them."

"How about a warrant for material witness?"

"That's a little thin, even for a big city boy like you. We might have to wait until we can connect some physical evidence."

Charlie thought for a moment. "How about Judge Wooten?"

Whittaker shook his head and scuffed his shoes on the ground while he thought. "You sure like swimming in shark infested waters, don't you."

"Already in up to my neck." Charlie pulled out the judge's business card and handed it to him. "When you call him, tell him I said that no beans have been spilled."

Arnie looked at the card before taking it and asking, by his surprised expression, how the hell the private dick from Chicago got Judge Wooten's business card. Wordlessly, he pulled out his cell phone and moved away from the group so as not to be heard.

Charlie, too, moved away and started walking toward the running creek. He needed some head clearance, and some respite from the flies and other insects that had started to be attracted by all the warm bodies working around the wreck. When he got about a hundred yards east, he found a spot on the bank that gave him a good view of the farm to the south. The farmer seemed to be sorting his cows into two different pens. Beyond the barns, Charlie could see parked equipment and still further away a farm house with a front porch covered with morning glories. He took a deep breath and tried to gather some relaxation from the bucolic scene.

It wasn't more than ten minutes before the medical examiner sat down beside him. "Mind?" asked Thomas.

"Naw. It may be good for me to bounce a few things off somebody other than Arnie Whittaker anyway."

"What's on your mind?" Thomas pulled up a stalk of rye and started chewing on the end.

"Have we missed anything?"

"Hell. I won't even be able to tell you 'til we can move the body back to the morgue."

Charlie shook his head. "No. I mean with Flatwood and the other guy. Is there anything you can do that you haven't done?"

"Sure hope not." Thomas kept chewing the rye for a long time. "It seems like we only have one of two murder weapons."

"So you think that the tire iron from Frederickson's trunk is going to match the Indian's wounds?"

"Like I said, ninety percent."

Charlie was silent for a long time, then asked, "Why would a smart guy like Frederickson keep a murder weapon?" It was a rhetorical question. Charlie had already fixed on the theory that he was holding it for blackmail against somebody else.

Just as Reed Thomas was about to answer, they both started a bit at the two gunshots that seemed to come from the area of the farm. Charlie gave the AME a concerned look, but Thomas just said, "Smart people do stupid things." As an answer to the detective's rhetorical question, it was as useful a theory as anything. He looked around and discovered that nobody seemed concerned about the gunshots. Thomas sensed his concern and said, "We're out in the country. Farmer's son could be shooting rats."

"That sounded like a shotgun."

"Big rats."

"Okay," Charlie said. "On the subject of shooting in general. What do you make of the shooter on Frederickson?"

"Don't quote me on this, because I haven't had the chance to get any lab work done." Charlie nodded his assent and Thomas went on. "Something out of a deer rifle with a scope, like a 243 or a 308 with a ballistic tip. Or maybe even a full metal jacket. It's not a terrible wound, so the round probably didn't blow up or expand significantly past the entrance wound."

"With a deer rifle like that," Charlie speculated. "How far away would the muzzle have to be before it wouldn't leave any splatter burns?"

"Anything from across a room to a hundred feet."

"Have you ever seen a marksman who could hit a head-sized target moving horizontally at seventy to eighty? That's a mighty good shot. Or the shooter was a lot closer."

"Would be a lot tougher at a hundred feet," the AME noted. "The swing in the barrel alone would be unmanageable."

Just as Charlie was about to speak again, another two shots came from across the river. Charlie stood up and saw the farmer in one of his pens. A third shot followed. "That farmer's shooting his own cattle? Why would he do that?"

Thomas was unfazed. "You really never lived on a farm, have you?"

"City boy, through and through. It's tattooed on my butt cheeks."

Thomas stood up. "He's either putting down some diseased head, or he's going to dress them and have one hell of a barbecue this Fourth of July."

"Shooting? I thought they banged them over the head with a mallet."

"He's using a captive bolt gun. Drive's the bolt just far enough into the brain to kill without ruining the 'parts is parts' parts." Charlie looked at him as though he'd had a sudden revelation. "Thought of that. But Danny didn't have any powder burns. A bolt gun would have left more burns on human flesh than a normal handgun at close range."

Both men started walking back to the accident scene. The afternoon sun had gotten low enough in the west that the trees threw shadows almost back to the clearing where they had been sitting. Most of the crime team still bustled around the vehicle and the dead body. Pictures and measurements were being made in every conceivable direction. A group of about a dozen uniforms still wandered along the right of way to the west. They had made it almost back up to the nose of the IS250 when Thomas asked, "What did you mean about a close shot?"

"I was thinking more like a shot taken from a moving vehicle, right alongside the Lexus."

"The shooter would have to have an accomplice."

"Not necessarily. There was a movie stunt car driver that used to do fairs and carnivals around the Midwest who used to shoot out a series of beer kegs – not with real beer – from his car going about ninety. One man operation. No sidekick. Used a 30-30. Had some kind of sling arrangement hanging from the roof on the passenger side. I never saw it up close, but that's what I'm wondering here."

Thomas thought for awhile. "If that were true, then the bullet would have forward momentum, just like the car. After a clean shot thru a moving target, it would still have forward momentum. We're looking too far west for the slug!"

Sgt. Whittaker had been talking to a couple of crime scene technicians, but, seeing them both, walked over. "We've got the warrants," he said to Charlie, ignoring

Thomas' efforts to speak first. "But we didn't get 'em from Wooten. His fill-in said the good judge had gotten a headache and let everyone know he wasn't taking any calls."

Charlie decided that he'd let the new bullet trajectory be AME Thomas' idea. "That's great news," he said. "But Thomas has something to tell you." Whittaker looked from Charlie to Thomas.

"We need to have the uniforms search for the slug much, much closer to here. And much further down into the wash there. In fact, have them look in the creek bed."

Whittaker left to find the state trooper in charge, and AME Thomas got on his cell phone about the lab results on the tire iron, leaving Charlie to think a bit more about how he wanted to play this. Charlie hoped that the word on the lab results was good, but even if it wasn't, he had a gut feeling that he was close to the truth. When Whittaker came back, he asked who they had sent to pick up the witnesses and told Whittaker that he preferred that the troopers bring both Margaret and Liz to the scene without having any conversations with them, even casual. "Better they don't know who's under the drop cloth." He also suggested a few places that they might look for the two women, including the bed and breakfast where he had seen them hole up the night before.

"Good news," yelled Thomas as he ran back toward the two men. "The blood is a good match to Danny's. We've got one of our murder weapons."

"Any prints?" Whittaker beat Charlie on that question.

"Two different latents. They're running them now. Any of our suspects that you think won't be in the database?"

Charlie had an idea. "Just in case, Arnie, if they haven't picked up the witnesses yet, see if their lieutenant thinks his men are smart enough to get prints without the ladies knowing   it."

"Should be a piece of cake. I think all the troopers have tablet computers now."

To Thomas, Charlie said, "I imagine DNA will take longer?"

"Fifteen hours to get a good enough match to stand up in court," said the AME. "And that's rushing it."

"Okay. Now we wait."

Before the sun set on the crime scene, Charlie thought he had the investigation under control. The AME's office brought in a dozen floodlights to illuminate the important spots, and had them running as the sun went down. Night would never come to Gromer Frederickson on his last day on earth. The lights were a fitting metaphor for what Charlie thought he had done for the case in general. This had gone from a case in which the lead investigator thought a couple of drunk college punks had done two people just to get some free tires for their sweet rides to one that involved a cover-up of stock manipulation and a high-profile suspect with a lot to hide. Shedding light was all he could do. The cops would still have to make the case.

The night got darker, until the areas surrounding the crime scene were invisible from anywhere within the perimeter. Charlie's doubts got darker, too. Would Margaret really hire a stunt man to kill Frederickson? He could easily see Margaret or Liz wielding a tire iron, but he still didn't understand how one of them could have put the bolt into Danny's skull? Were the flat tire murders done by two people? And could the trick shot that killed Frederickson be self-protection? The man he was out to "take care of," in Margaret's words, was a mild mannered pharmacist who knew too much. Or was he?

The police van carrying Margaret Trapp-Segundo and Elizabeth Wallace pulled up about an hour past sunset. Whittaker had arranged to debrief the driver, just in case any conspiracies had been hatched between the two women while in custody. Charlie and the rest of the plainclothes people drifted off into the shadows to watch. He noticed that, even thought it seemed pitch dark from inside the harsh lighting, the western sky still showed pink, purple and blue fading to black as the stars over Eastern Iowa started to twinkle overhead. The frogs and the insects had set up a cacophony that rivaled the trucks running past. The truck traffic had picked up to the point where almost no private vehicles were using the Interstate.

Charlie noticed that the uniform had to drag Margaret out of the van and stay behind her to make her walk toward the body. Liz, on the other hand, got out willingly and more or less tagged along. Both had their hands held behind them by cable ties that had been loosely applied, as Whittaker had ordered. He didn't want one of them to kill themselves by panicking and running without their arms free to balance. Applied this way, the ties would make them think twice, a kind of "we're watching you" reminder. It appeared to Charlie, however, that neither was going to try bolting, and both were ready to play the game.

Another thing that Charlie noticed: the great lengths to which both women went to make it appear that they didn't know each other, let alone that they were on intimate footing. Margaret, still in the clothes she had on when she had met with Charlie early that day, repeatedly turned to look at the uniform while walking. She never let he eyes meet Liz's, and, whenever Liz walked a little closer to her, she quickly adjusted and moved to her left to keep the uniform between them. Liz had on a leather jacket that looked too big for her, like something she had borrowed, and a pair of tight blue jeans. For the most part, she kept looking down at the ground as they walked, never up to see where she was being guided, and never to her left, where Margaret walked.

Only as they got closer to the corpse under the tarp, and Liz could no longer avoid the sight simply by looking down, did she direct a long, pleading look at Liz. To Charlie, her look said, "Whatever or whoever this is, will you still be with me?" An answer wasn't returned.

As the trio of Liz, Margaret, and the officer stopped at the edge of the pool of light illuminating the remains, Reed Thomas emerged from the shadows and lifted a corner of the tarp to reveal Frederickson's mangled head. Liz immediately took a step back and caught herself, trying unsuccessfully to raise a hand to her face and instead getting her wrist only half out of the cable tie. Margaret stood stoically, as if she'd just been shown a patch of dandelions or a pile of used tires. When Thomas asked them to identify the body, only Margaret spoke, and just the name of the man with whom she had been passionate only that morning. No longer hungry when the soup is cold, thought Charlie.

On a simple hand signal from Thomas, another uniform brought over a picture of the bloody tire iron, and Reed held it in the light in front of the women. Again, Margaret stood unmoved and shook her head no. Liz came apart within seconds, collapsing forward in a faint and landing with her face almost against the bloody head. Thomas almost immediately began efforts to revive her.

"So now what?" The question came from Whittaker, who had been standing next to Charlie and silently watching the spectacle.

"Question them."

"We'll have to take your client in for medical attention." The observation was flat and Whittaker knew the answer.

"Then question my client at the hospital."

"Is she still your client?"

"We'll see."

Chapter Ten

He knew that there would be no questioning of suspects that night. It was well past eleven by the time the paramedics were through with Liz Wallace and she was on her way to the University of Iowa Hospital with a police escort. Charlie had decided not to confront Margaret before they loaded her, too – with much protestation about the prowess of her lawyers – into the police van. He found his rental in the dark and, exhausted and still wearing the clothes he had left Iowa City with almost 36 hours before, got in. His cell phone started playing Sinatra and he looked at it. It was Linda.

"Nice digs," she said when he answered. "Where are you?"

"Halfway between Des Moines and Iowa City, and on my way back," he lied. He had planned to get off at the next truck stop and take a nap. "Where the hell are you?"

167

"Nice! I don't hear from you in three days and what I get from you is profanity?"

Charlie laughed and responded, "Okay. Tell me where the hell you are, Sweetheart, please?"

"That's better. I'm in your motel room. That's why I said, nice digs. I had to pay the guy at the desk fifty to let me in here. I thought I'd come out for the weekend and surprise you. Tomorrow's Saturday, you know." Then she stopped and said, "That's right. You wouldn't."

It would be a half-gallon of coffee instead of a nap, he thought, and said, "Listen, Doll, I think I'm going to be busy tomorrow morning."

"Then I'm going to see that you're busy tonight, too. If you ever get your sweet hot ass back to this motel room." It was an invitation he couldn't refuse. "What's your ETA?"

"If I ain't there by one, you can start without me, if you know what I mean."

Satisfied, shaved, brushed, showered, and, yet again satisfied, Charlie parked the little rental Focus in the police lot and whistled as he got out. He felt good in a light polo shirt and a pair of summer weight slacks that Linda had brought with her from Chicago. She knew he never packed right for his cases. The air was almost Central Illinois warm – too warm for nine in the morning – with the promise of humidity and an afternoon thunderstorm. Bees buzzed happily in the gardens that had been planted around the city building and made random passes at the smell of his aftershave, also a Chicago export thanks to Linda. He really hoped to get this over with and get back to her, but was happy that, in less than an hour, the local shopping mall would open and she'd have something to occupy her time.

He'd taken two calls on his hurried way back to the motel and to Linda, both calls while making ninety to a hundred and juggling the phone and his jumbo TA trucker's coffee. The hag behind the counter had offered to sell him a case of Red Bull. "You need it, buddy." He hadn't needed it when he got to his motel. And to Linda. The first call had been from Arnie Whittaker, who wanted to schedule the interrogation of Margaret Trapp for eight, a squad meeting at nine, and a visit to Charlie's client in the hospital at ten. "Make it nine, ten, and eleven, and I'm in," he'd answered. He learned that Liz had been dehydrated and anemic in addition to her other problems.

Another mile or two and he'd taken a call from Reed Thomas. "The prints on the tire iron match Liz Wallace's prints from the state trooper's computer." There it was, another problem for Liz Wallace. She had hired him to solve a murder that she had committed.

He hadn't wanted to think about it on the way back in, but despite his good mood, he was thinking now. How the hell did Liz Wallace get that bolt into Danny's head? How did Margaret and her sales lackey fit into it, and who had taken the trick shot that killed the bastard? He wondered if Whittaker would still be willing to interrogate Margaret, or if the threats of litigation from her attorneys would take their toll. Even Whittaker would have to figure out some of these questions in order to convict Charlie's client for all three murders, and there had been a whole night for Margaret's people to do their string pulling.

After getting buzzed into the inner sanctum, Charlie was met in the hallway by both Whittaker and Lt. Breitling. "The interrogation of Margaret Trapp is off," said Breitling. It sounded like an order to Charlie. "And I don't appreciate the end run you did with Judge Wooten. His backup is already asking questions. That was shaky police work, and you know it. It was only a matter of time before we had Trapp lawyers all over us."

"Has she already refused the interview?" Charlie could see that he was going to need to go for the Hail Mary.

"Not in so many words." Through all this, Arnie looked at his shoes. He'd been given a dressing down by his boss, the way Charlie saw it, so he didn't have an ally. "But Trapp attorneys are over at the courthouse right now getting a WHC. What harebrained nonsense are you up to now?

"You've got security cameras in here, don't you?" He didn't wait for an answer. "Come outside and I'll tell you."

They walked all the way out to Charlie's rental car. Breitling got into the front with Charlie and Whittaker squeezed into the back. As Breitling closed his door, he said, "This had better be good."

Charlie told them about his stumbling into Jimmy's and his fortuitous opportunity to stake out Margaret and Liz two nights before. Leaving out Judge Wooten, he then told of his opportunity to do some "reconnaissance" at Trapp Tire. When he had finished, Breitling looked stunned. Through the rear view mirror, Charlie could see that Whittaker thought it was hilarious. Breitling rubbed his chin and mused, "That certainly would put Margaret in the role of a co-conspirator." He popped open the door. "Whittaker, go find out what judge they're seeing over there, and tell the judge we've got a legitimate charge now."

"Wait!" Charlie put a hand out to Breitling. "As soon as we tell the judge, her attorneys will tell her, and I lose any leverage I have with her."

Whittaker piped up. "We could go to a different judge, and then we'd have dueling warrants, and we'd have to go to a third judge to sort it out. In the mean time, we wouldn't have to release her."

Charlie thought a moment. "What about Liz Wallace?"

"She's already under arrest at the hospital and been given her rights. She hasn't made a statement. She will." Whittaker seemed confident.

"You okay with this?" It was directed at Lt. Breitling.

"You've got two hours. If I think this thing is going downhill by then, I'm pulling the plug and giving Ms.Trapp-Segundo an apology and a free ride home. You got that?"

The University Police detachment they had put on his client didn't blink twice at the ICPD badge when Charlie asked to be let into her room at University Hospital. Liz wouldn't have known his part in her arrest, and she brightened visibly at his arrival. Without makeup and a combing out, though, she looked ten years older and very, very tired. An IV ran into her right arm, and he wondered if AME Thomas had thought of checking whether the fingerprints were positioned for a right- or left-handed blow. Charlie thought about the sexy, mysterious woman who had come to his office to accuse the person he now understood to be her cousin of a murder she had committed. Or had she? It weighed on her hard now, but why hadn't it then? It still hadn't weighed on her when she had tried to seduce him in his motel room.

Finding no convenient chair on his side of the small room, a private one where she had been moved after her arrest, he pulled an exam stool from a corner and rolled it over. He sat leaning over the edge of the thick hospital mattress as she looked at him without flinching. "Hello, Liz."

She smiled at him, and he felt guilty. She still thought he was on her side. "This isn't how it was supposed to go," she said weakly. She put out her hand to touch his sleeve, and he took it in his and held it hard.

"Okay, Babe. The cops that count don't know I'm here, and I've got about twenty minutes, so tell me how it was supposed to go."

"She said he was supposed to protect me."

"Who and from what?"

"Margaret's guy. The big salesman." Did she somehow know he knew of their relationship?

"Again I ask: From what?"

"I'm afraid now. They'll kill me!"

"Listen, Sister. Right now the cops have enough evidence against you to put you away for at least second-degree murder. So tell me who 'they' are, or I might just take out a contract on you myself."

She tried to pull her hand away, but he just held it tighter. Tears started to form in the corners of her eyes, which were red from the last spate. "I did kill him," she whimpered. "I just saw the way to get out and I killed him, and then they were there, and they threatened to go to the police if I didn't take care of it."

"You killed the Indian?"

"He was going to rape me."

"Seth Sharedream was going to rape you? Right in the middle of Danny's tire store?"

She nodded and choked back a sob. "Right there with Danny."

"Danny was alive?"

Before she could answer, her eyes got wider, as though she was seeing something that scared the crap out of her. Her mouth opened and moved a few times, not in words but like a fish out of water. Then she relaxed and her eyes closed? "Liz,

Liz?" Charlie yelled and shook her. This wasn't right, even if she had been sedated. Sedatives don't work like that.

He checked the IV for signs of tampering, and, finding none, yanked the needle out of her arm. Turning on his heels, he banged open the door, ran into the hall and yelled for a nurse. The two "unicops" at the door looked surprised. The younger black cop rushed to follow Charlie to the nurse's station, and the other ducked into Liz's room. When he was sure there was a blue-jacketed nurse high-tailing it to the room, Charlie turned on the cop. "Has anyone been in that room besides hospital personnel?"

The cop still looked surprised, and Charlie could see sweat on his forehead. "No, sir. Only one on this watch was that male nurse about a half hour ago."

"Male nurse?" The question came from an older, black female nurse behind the desk.

"Yeah. White guy about my height? Glasses? Mustache? He had an ID badge."

The nurse stood up to her full height, which was taller than either of the two men. "Son, there ain't no male nurses on this shift. And there ain't no male nurses with face hair in this whole danged hospital. Nursing supervisor is real tight-assed about that. And we gave your chief a personnel list. Can't you read, boy?" She threw her pen on the desk and ambled toward Liz's room to see what was going on. "Ain't fit to be no cop at a Walmart," she mumbled.

The unicop looked at Charlie for some kind of absolution, and Charlie just said, "Let's just hope I got the IV out in time." He pulled out his phone to call the real cops.

Whittaker's first reaction was to upbraid Charlie for going in to talk to Liz Wallace without his permission. The he turned to the "unicop" sergeant, his counterpart, who had been angrily questioning his own officers about the unidentified nurse imposter. "Let's have both your men go over to ICPD and work on the sketch program. I'd like to see the face of whoever is trying to kill my suspects."

"Not kill, Officer." The lanky intern who had just come out of Liz's room walked over to them. "I think your assailant was grasping at straws, but this wouldn't have killed her." He held up a gloved hand with an empty pill bottle labeled as Methotrexate.

"Where'd you find that." Whittaker took a close look to confirm it was empty.

"On the floor in the corner next to the IV stand."

Charlie asked, "How bad is it?

"This is a pretty strong cancer drug that can also mess with your immune system," the young doctor said. "I don't think it was the IV. I think he put it in the water pitcher. One of the side effects, especially in patients with too high a dose, is disorientation. Another is syncope, which you witnessed. Sudden LOC. Lights out."

Whittaker called a crime scene tech over to get the bottle. "And have it checked for anything other than what it says on the label. We don't know what we're dealing with here."

"Where did that bottle come from?" Charlie asked the intern.

"Beats me. We don't even have a cancer unit in this building. Maybe it was stolen from the cancer center, but I doubt it. They order these drugs only for when they have a patient coming in. It's a matter of keeping the costs down by not stocking expensive drugs with short shelf life. I'd guess they came from a private supply."

"Can that happen?"

"If, you've got enough money." The intern looked around and said. "I've got to get back to my patients. Anything else?" He left before Whittaker could answer.

Charlie stood around thinking about how they would go about finding a suspect with cancer and enough money to buy a private pharmacy. Whittaker, in the mean time, called to see how the dueling warrants were doing. "We've got a warrant for criminal conspiracy on the strength of your statement," he finally told Charlie.

"Did Link Sheffield ever have cancer?" It was an honest question.

"That whiny druggist never had anything, catching or not. I don't know if you looked at it, but his financial in the case file shows that he's got more debt than the United States Treasury. That pharmacy of his belongs to four different banks, all of 'em ready to board it up and turn the property into a Chuck E. Cheese."

"We need to talk to Margaret before she gets another round of lawyers to post bail."

The night in jail had done almost as bad a number on Margaret Trapp as the night in the hospital had done on her lover. They hadn't let her keep her dress, now that she was actually under arrest, and the grey jump suit that said PRISONER front and back didn't flatter her a bit. She sat across from Charlie and Arnie Whittaker in the same room where Charlie had interviewed Owen Barside – what was it? – three days before. Her dark hair had been combed out – shower, search and fumigate – and pulled back into a ponytail held by piece of string. Without all of her expensive makeup, she was truly homely.

Charlie opened with a wisecrack he couldn't resist. "Well, at least with your hair like that we know that the wig was the blonde." Margaret shot him a fuck-you look and Whittaker tugged on his arm to suggest that he not continue along that line. He looked at Whittaker and back to her. "You know why you've been arrested?"

"Do you know why I have enough money to buy this shit-assed police department six times over?"

"I'd say you screwed your way into it. And you didn't care who or what it was you were screwing." He jumped back away from the table as she made an attempt to lunge at him but was held back by the handcuffs holding her in the chair. "Little sensitive?"

She just glared at him, and Whittaker asked, "Why don't you let me try?"

"Suit yourself."

"Missus Segundo," Arnie started. "Did you know that, about forty minutes ago, somebody tried to kill Elizabeth Wallace in her hospital bed?"

Her shoulders sagged. "Is she okay? Is she . . . What do you mean tried?"

"An unsuccessful attempt to poison her. The details don't matter. But talkin' to her, I get the impression that she's afraid of something or somebody so important that maybe both of you are in danger." He let it sink in for a few seconds. "Meet any interesting people in lockup last night?"

Charlie could see the wheels turning, and she finally said, "Can you keep this out of the papers?"

"Give me a reason."

"Because the people she's afraid of would love to find out that you have the CEO of Trapp Tire in your crummy little jail."

"Stock traders?" Charlie interjected. "People who would like to see Trapp tire take a nosedive for one reason or another? But how about a name?"

"She never gave me a name. She never had a chance."

"Sure looked like you had a chance the other night." He paused for impact. "You girls could have exchanged a lot more than names from the action I was seeing."

Again, Whittaker tried to keep control of the situation. "Just tell us what she did tell you."

"The day it happened. You know?"

"The murders?"

"Yes. The day the murders happened, Liz came to my office in the afternoon. She was out of her mind. I don't know if she had taken some pills, and I hoped to God she hadn't driven her car all the way from Iowa City. To look at her, she had just seen her dog run over by a garbage truck or something."

"But it was worse than that, wasn't it." Charlie shifted in his seat.

"Much worse. She told me she had to hit some guy over the head with a tire iron to keep from getting raped. And there were witnesses who could do things much worse to her than just putting her in jail."

"Witnesses? She said more than one?"

"Yes, I specifically remember her saying that."

"Go on."

"I asked her what she was doing at the tire store, and she said that she'd gotten a call from Nordella Flatwood, or, more exactly from Nordella's phone. There was no message, but it was followed by a text asking her to meet Nordella there that morning. Anyway, she said she got there and was confronted by the Indian, who wouldn't take no for an answer. She said she just went nuts and grabbed a tire iron and started swinging. Before she knew it, the Indian was on the floor and the witness was standing there – this time she said witness, singular - telling her that she had done a very bad thing, but they could fix it for her. She ran and didn't stop running until she got to my office."

Whittaker looked at Charlie. "We're getting a warrant to search her car. Maybe the other weapon is in there as well."

Margaret looked concerned. "She never said anything about the other man, my dealer, Mr. Flatwood. Only about the Indian."

"Which brings us back around to why you're under arrest. You've admitted to conspiring to cover up a homicide and to conceal evidence. We assume you assigned your crackerjack salesman, the now deceased Mr. Frederickson, to assist Ms. Wallace in covering up the crime. That would explain why he had the tire iron in his car. When he found out that he had physical evidence that he could use against both of you, he was going to sell it to the highest bidder. Except one of the bidders paid with a bad check." Whittaker paused to let it sink in, and Charlie stretched as if wanting to get the interrogation over with and get back to his client.

But Whittaker continued, "You're also here because you had motive to want Danny Flatwood and his informal business partner Link Sheffield as cold and dead as poor Mr. Sharedream. We have reason to believe you ordered Frederickson to do something about Mr. Sheffield. Did that include murder?"

"As I told Mr. Komensky here, Gromer was good at only two things. One was spending my money to make people do what I wanted, and the other one wasn't murder. He was a lover, not a killer."

The puzzled look on Whittaker's face made Charlie lean over and whisper the answer in his ear. "All three?" Charlie nodded yes. Whittaker shook his head and turned back to Margaret. "So no names?"

"She may have told Gromer, but not me."

Charlie's phone rang, but he ignored it. "You do realize this puts you in danger? You should watch your back. We may have to put you in solitary for your own protection until we sort this out." Turning to Whittaker, he asked, "Anything else?"

"We know there are one or two witnesses and they are either important or powerful or both, if these upstanding ladies are to be believed. So I guess not."

Just then Charlie's phone rang again. The caller ID said it was Linda, so he flipped the phone open and took it.

Chapter Eleven

In a panic situation. That's when Charlie thought most clearly. It had stood him in good stead as a cop, and it had saved his life a number of times. Dumb luck had saved it a number of times more. Luck, as in getting out of the Mustang before the bomb went off. Luck, as in having enough plastic baggies in the car for an extra few breaths of air.

As he roared along in the Focus with the speedometer pegged at 90 and hoping that Whittaker had had enough sense to just warn troopers to let him go and do what he had to do, he felt clear enough in the head to know that this was luck too. Bad luck. Why the hell had she decided to visit for the weekend? Didn't she think he had his hands full? Of course she didn't. Despite what he usually went through on a case, his job seemed to her more like glamour and vacation than like high risk and sleepless nights.

Then again, clearly thinking, he couldn't blame her. Whoever had taken Linda had been watching him, and had the manpower to watch her, too. Whoever, had taken Linda probably had killed Danny Flatwood and Gromer Frederickson and made an attempt on the life of the only remaining person who knew his or her identity.

He couldn't have waited to interview Liz Wallace. The call he had picked up had been from Linda's phone, but it wasn't Linda. A husky, male, obviously disguised voice – the disguised male voices were always husky – had simply said to go to the Sheffield farm and the woman wouldn't be harmed. Trite and cliché – the villains always were that, too – but scary enough for him to take Whittaker aside and ask him where the Sheffield farm was located. The answer: "Which one?" It panicked him a little bit more.

He had thought there was something about the pharmacist and his relationship with the tire dealer. He hadn't been able to put his finger on it, but it gelled sometime after his talk with AME Thomas the night before, when Thomas took for granted the strange device the farmer was using to slaughter his cattle. The Sheffield's were a cattle farming family. He didn't know how Sheffield had done it without powder burns, but why was he speeding to the third of four possible Sheffield farms if he didn't think Link Sheffield was his man?

"I've got a tip," he had answered. "Maybe a murder weapon." That was all he had told Whittaker. With Arnie's help, they had tracked down the ag properties that belonged to Sheffield's family. All six of them. He knew that if he had told the cop that a citizen was being held against her will that two things would have happened, in his mind neither of them good. The first would have been the involvement of the FBI. The second would have been Charlie being physically restrained from going to the Sheffield farm, whichever Sheffield farm it was.

Charlie found it odd for his mind to have thought of calling Linda to start calling Sheffields in the area to eliminate some of the possible locations. Funny how the mind works when you get too used to rely on somebody always being there. Had managed to eliminate two of the possibilities with his own phone calls before he screeched out of the police parking lot and turned the heads of a few officers who had been loitering on breaks.

That left four farms, and by going the wrong direction twice, interviewing the farmers and convincing himself that nothing nefarious was going on in the old cow barn, he was down to two. Ag properties and cow barns. He'd already learned not to call them farms. Ag properties belonged to either growers or breeders, and there were several kinds of barns. He filed it away for future use and decided that the next case he took would be somewhere within Chicago city limits. Now he was doing ninety on County Road W55. Ninety wasn't safe. Why did Sheffield have to have a farm on a winding road?

There were some things that just seemed wrong with the theory that Sheffield was his perp. It was true that Sheffield was basically broke and mortgaged to the hilt. If he had somebody powerful helping him, why was he so concerned that the rubber formula be a success? If the family pervert Bicklin Harding was helping him, he had a sweet deal. Even though it wasn't a success, he was going to get paid off by the big salesman. The rumored tire formula was going to hold up the value of the Trapp Tire stock along with the holding company that Grandpa Pervert had money in. Win and win again. Maybe not as much money, but enough. No, there had to be something more. Something he was missing.

Damn it! He caught sight of a milepost and it told him he still had about five miles to go. He wasn't going to call

Linda's phone until he was very close, and then, if it answered, he was going to ask for more time to get there. It wouldn't give him much of an edge, but he hoped for a little surprise factor.

He thought again about all of the other people he had interacted with since arriving in Iowa City. Could any of them be his perpetrator? Before he had time to sort it out, his phone rang and identified Linda. He grabbed it. "Hello? Linda?"

He couldn't understand the husky voice over the road roar. "What?"

The sudden impact startled him and he realized something had hit the windshield. It cracked badly and the cracks spread fast, but he could still see. Before he could throw the phone down onto the passenger seat a heavy thump sent the Focus turning hard right. He grabbed the steering wheel but knew that, at this speed, control wasn't going to happen. Just before the Focus went into the roll, he caught a glimpse of the big, black vehicle coming toward him. The son of a bitch had come out to meet him on the way.

He'd been in rollovers before, but this one was bad. The trick was to keep your neck from snapping and hope the restraints held well enough to keep you in the car. He pushed his head against the headrest and tried counting, but lost count when the third bounce whipped his head forward and sideways against the side pillar. Air bags were all over the place. The lights went out.

He came to with no vision whatsoever. He was in a seated position on a chair with no armrests and his hands secured to his sides by something that at first felt like a wide band around his chest and his abdomen. He tried moving his fingers and found that his left hand hurt like hell and his right seemed okay. His neck felt like the muscles around his spine had grown six sizes and were holding his head almost like a big collar. Even the slightest movement of his head – up, down, right, back – caused extreme pain. He wiggled his toes and could feel them in his shoes. At least, if he had broken anything, his spinal cord was still communicating. Then his vision started coming back, nothing but a blur at first, and then what light there was became too intense and he closed his eyes.

It seemed like natural light. Good that he hadn't been out too long. Just long enough to get him into this mess, he thought. He also discovered that his legs were bound together and to the chair, so to stand seemed useless for the moment. He opened his eyes again and fought the pain that swelled into his forehead and made him want to close them. The light came through vertical slits – the spaces between vertical barn boards. He was in a barn.

Crap! thought Charlie. I hope there's no livestock wandering around in here in the dark. But the smells were just of hay and dirt. Maybe a storage barn. "Linda?" he called tentatively.

To his surprise, her voice came out of the darkness. Rather it was her voice muffled by something, probably a gag. "Ummph." He wondered why they hadn't put a gag on him. They wanted him to know she was there.

"You okay?"

"Ummm, hummm." He heard it as a positive. Her voice turned up at the end. But the inside of the mostly empty barn didn't give him much directional hearing. And one ear was ringing from the probable head injury that had put him out for how long he didn't know.

"Do you know how many there are?

"Ummm, ummm." That was negative.

He went through a few more simple questions, and found out that she had been knocked out, but probably only from some kind of drug, that she was restrained in a similar way, and that she could not tell where he was in the barn relative to her. She had not seen her assailants and couldn't tell him where they were. He assumed it was the Sheffield farm, but had nothing to back up the assumption. His head pounded with every beat of his heart, and sounds were starting to be more painful to his ears, or at least to his good ear. The extreme tinnitus continued in the other. But his eyes had started to adjust to the light.

He gave himself and Linda a few more seconds to relax, after which he was certain he could see moving light coming off something like smooth leather. Moving like breathing. She was off to his right and about twenty feet away – assuming it was her. Could he drag the chair over to her? Was it her, or somebody else unconscious? Who else had Link Sheffield kidnapped?

The answer came in a crash of splintering wood, shattering glass, and exploding clouds of dust. Directly in front of him and within a few feet of where he had perceived the other, breathing presence, the black SUV had crashed through the barn wall, taking down half of the framing with it and scattering debris at his feet. The daylight that burst through the wall along with the SUV revealed that there was, indeed, a third kidnap victim. Link Sheffield sat in another chair, unconscious, bound by leather straps and livestock tape. His head lolled sideways and a bad wound that appeared to go right through his right cheek dripped blood onto his white pharmacist's tunic. As Charlie squinted, trying to see who was in the SUV, he heard Linda's still-gagged voice now clearly coming from behind him. "I'm okay!" he yelled.

"I wouldn't be too sure about that." The voice belonged to the man getting out of the driver's side of the SUV, and Charlie still tried to adjust his eyes to the penetrating daylight that got even more intense and annoying as the dust settled. The man looked up at a section of the unsupported, damaged roof that dangled above the SUV. "Looks like this old barn might collapse on you three at any minute."

Rafe Flatwood! Looking older and rougher than when Charlie had pushed him into the pool, he grinned and pointed to the sagging timbers with the hunting rifle that he held carelessly in this left hand. His black hair was full cut and hung loosely over his ears, not slicked back by the water as Charlie remembered it. He wore tight black denim jeans with cowboy boots and a loose-fitting faux suede shirt. A young man, thought Charlie. A young, rich man who knew how to make himself look attractive and dangerous at the same time.

"Judging from the vehicle you're driving, I would say that you're not too interested in rescuing any of us from that," observed Charlie.

Rafe took up a classic cowboy pose with his left leg cocked forward and the rifle, pointing upward, nested easily against his left hip. It was then that Charlie noticed the odd looking firearm in an equally odd holster on which the boy rested his right hand. "Wouldn't have had to rescue no one if you had just minded your own business, mister private dick."

"Do you still think you're protecting your mother?"

"Hell, no, you stupid piece of crap." The boy spat out the words. "I knew who killed my father and the Indian from the start." Without saying another word, Rafe walked off in the direction where Charlie had heard Linda's voice.

"What are you going to do? Leave her alone!" He struggled against the pain of his injured neck and tried to turn and see Linda.

"I'm not going to do anything to her unless I know you're watching, old man." Charlie heard scuffling and a few muffled groans and grunts from Linda, and Rafe soon walked back into the light with Linda in a fireman's carry over his right shoulder. Bound with her arms and legs in the same leather straps as on Sheffield, and with her shirt torn open to reveal her bra, her jeans dusty and covered with pieces of straw, she struggled and grunted until he threw her down hard onto the ground. She landed on her butt and groaned and rolled over on her side. "See, I told you I wanted you to see."

Sadists, particularly smug ones, really pissed Charlie off. Had he been free at that moment, he probably would have strangled the boy with his bare hands. But the situation called for a calm, reasoned approach. He needed to see if the boy could be defused. "I'm sure you had a good reason for killing your father," he guessed.

Rafe's head almost robotically snapped to attention in Charlie's direction, and he lowered the rifle, still controlled by his left hand, so Charlie could see down the barrel. "What do you know, old man?"

"I know you're a good son and you love your mother. So whatever reason you had to kill Danny, he must have done something unforgivable to her."

Rafe swiveled and swung the muzzle of the rifle over until it was almost against Sheffield's still unconscious head. "That's what he said."

Charlie wasn't surprised, but asked, "He knew?"

Rafe Chuckled, and then sarcastically said, "Uncle Link. The poor bastard is so starved for both friendship and cash that he was willing to do things to cast suspicion his own way to help me out. All I had to do was tell him how much money my pervert Grandfather would throw his way, and how I'd be his lifelong friend 'til death do us part." He swung the rifle back in Charlie's direction, then pointed it at the ceiling again. While he did this, Charlie noticed that Linda had managed to get herself sitting upright, and was just a short way behind Rafe from Charlie's vantage point. "Did you know that Uncle Link invented the murder weapon?"

Charlie wanted to give Linda time to get into position. Linda was a shopkeeper in Oak Brook, but both of them had taken some martial arts training together, and he suspected she would know what to do when the moment was right. "Is that what you have there?" he asked.

"My dad gave him the idea. How about a bolt gun that could put down an ox without sounding like a gun shot. Runs on compressed air, like at the tire store. So Uncle Link could put down a head of beef right in the back room of his pharmacy, if he wanted to. It's against the law to discharge firearms in Iowa City."

Happy that he had succeeded in engaging the boy in conversation, Charlie decided the time was right to see if he could get a confession. "Want to tell me how it came to be a murder weapon?"

Rafe looked over his left shoulder at the unconscious pharmacist and over his right at Linda, who didn't shrink back but did her best to look unthreatening. "I borrowed it to show to dad that morning. His idea come to fruition. I knew he'd be tickled. Instead we got into it."

"About what?"

"No business of yours." Rafe sneered and lowered the rifle to point at Charlie's head again. "You don't need to know."

"Heard about your brother and your Grandpa." Charlie gambled that this would irritate Rafe even more, but instead he looked confused and cocked his head questioningly. Of course! Charlie realized that Rafe still thought nobody else knew the hideous family secret.

Linda saw this as an opportunity. She suddenly lashed out with both bound feet so as to plant her heels into the back of Rafe's right Achilles tendon. The blow caused him to yell in pain and he lost his footing, but surprisingly adeptly rolled between Sheffield and Charlie and recovered without losing his grip on the rifle. "You stupid bitch," he growled. "I should shoot you right here."

As Rafe raised the rifle, Charlie yelled, "Is that why you killed Danny? Did he know about the molesting?"

Cornered, Rafe Flatwood staggered back a few steps, limping on the damaged Achilles tendon. Charlie thought it was just because the boy didn't manage pain well. "He knew."

"And he wasn't going to turn Harding in."

"Not hardly. He was going to turn in my grandfather and ruin everything. He didn't understand. He didn't find out that the old fool had molested Junior until after Uncle Tim died. But I knew about it when Junior was six. I had it under control. We talked about it, little Danny and me. He had to talk about it. I told him that it wasn't right, but that going to Mom wouldn't fix things. I'd already heard family rumors, and I knew that Mom was as big a pervert as her old man. So I said to Danny, 'Kid, I know you're hurting and I know you've got a big burden of shame to get off your shoulders, but I guarantee you that if you let me handle it, you won't be sorry. When I finish school and start working for the company, I'll see to it that you and me get all the money. And then we'll bring the fucking bastard down.'

"We just had to wait another couple of years, and everything was going okay, and the Uncle Tim died and Dad got hooked up with this guy." He pointed to Link Sheffield.

"Did Sheffield what to get your grandfather's money?"

Rafe shrugged. "He knew Mom's family was rich, but he wanted to be friends more than he wanted something for nothing. He's an inventor. He just wanted an invention that worked and made him a lot of money. But he got friendly with Junior, too. And Junior had to go and tell him. I told him that talking to me was enough!" Rafe cried out the last sentence, almost in tears, and then took a deep breath and started again. "Uncle Link told Dad, and Dad wanted to turn Grandpa in right away, and that's what we argued about that morning at the store. I told Dad, 'Can't you see. If you turn him in there'll be scandal. It'll bring down the company and the stock of all the companies that Grandpa has an interest in. Uncle Link wants to make money off Uncle Link's rubber formula. The best revenge is for us to wait, and work to take down Grandpa from the inside.' But he wouldn't have any of it. He said that he was going to talk to the cops that day. There was a disconnected compressed air line on the floor. I could hear the compressors running.

"Before I knew it, I had the air hose in my hand and I made the connection with Uncle Link's invention. I needed a bolt, and the only thing I could see was the box of big screws for the racks. I grabbed one.

"Uncle Link's invention worked."

Rafe Flatwood suddenly became very silent and sullen looking. Fixing his jaw in a determined expression, he avoided making eye contact with Linda or with Charlie while checking the restraining leather straps on all three of his captives. After bustling around them each at least twice, he stopped, surveyed the scene – a triangle of three secured captives – and then walked out of the barn leaving the big, black SUV where he had gotten out of it.

Charlie knew immediately that this was Flatwood's big mistake. Though she was bruised and acting like she could hardly move, Linda was the only one of the three free to try to get around the place. Her eyes met Charlie's.

"I don't know how far the kid has gone," whispered Charlie. "But can you get me that piece of metal?" A piece of sheet metal that had been used long ago to patch a hole in the barn wall sat in the splinters close to the still unconscious pharmacist's feet. One edge had rusted enough that it would be thin, maybe sufficient enough to cut through the leather straps.

Linda nodded, and started moving herself towards Sheffield by pushing her heels out first, digging in and then trying to drag herself forward. She had to force her weight in the direction of her feet, bending at the waist as much as the leather bindings would allow. It could not have been easy, as Charlie heard her grunting both in physical exertion and in pain as she slowly inched her way to the metal. The trip took about five minutes, and, once she got the piece of metal firmly in her hands, getting to Charlie took at least another five. He could see the sweat breaking out on her forehead and on her bare neck as she inched closer. Her brown hair fell in tangles into her eyes, and he knew she suffered immensely.

Because he was still in the chair and she was on the ground with her hands effectively secured to her thighs, she had to turn herself over and try to get onto her knees to get the piece of metal into his hands, also effectively at his thighs. He had thought of tipping the chair on its side, but that would have immobilized one hand completely and just lifted the other one further out of her reach. Why did bindings seem the most diabolical when done in haste by a criminal who probably hadn't even thought about what he was doing?

"If you can get your mouth near me, I'll try to loosen the gag," he offered, but it was too late. At that moment, they both heard the putty putty sound from somewhere outside the barn. Charlie recognized it immediately as an industrial grade air compressor starting up. "Linda, he's coming!" This was not good. The compressor meant that he planned to use the bolt gun.

In haste, she rolled through the dust and splinters and bits of broken glass to get as far away from Charlie and back to her corner of the triangle as she could. But he had the piece of steel in his right hand and was slowly starting to use it on the binding that was next to his fingers.

Rafe appeared, dragging an air hose and looking critically at them. He saw Linda, covered in sweat and dirt and on her side almost where he had left her, and laughed. Then he said, "Didn't make much progress, did you honey?" Good! He had assumed she was still struggling to reach Charlie and hadn't even paused to consider what weapons might be found for them in the debris. Rafe deftly unholstered the strange gun and, with a loud hiss and a pop, engaged the air line. "It's a shame old Uncle Link went beserk," he mumbled.

Charlie watched as Rafe Flatwood managed the weapon and the air hose and cleaned both with a piece of red rag he'd pulled from his back pocket – red rag just like he'd used to gag Linda. Using the rag, the boy then cleanly pressed the weapon and the hose into Link Sheffield's limp right hand. As long as Charlie could see that Rafe was concentrating on making Link look like the murderer, he kept sawing away with the piece of steel. "Watch it, son," he said finally. "Maybe he's left handed."

Rafe looked at him and looked back at the inert Link Sheffield, searching desperately for some evidence that Link was right handed – doubting. And while Rafe was doubting, ultimately deciding to press Link's left hand against the gun as well, Charlie kept sawing. Out of the corner of his eye, Charlie could see that Linda was ready, and that she could see him nod. He'd gotten two straps cut through and needed time to get more.

The young Flatwood turned to Linda, holding the bolt gun, stainless bolt sticking partly out of what passed for a muzzle, using the rag to protect it from his own fingerprints. He'd done it backwards. He should have killed them first, then wiped the weapon, and that made Charlie confident that he had just enough doubt about killing Linda in cold blood that this would work. He had to start talking, and make it good. "You still haven't told me about the Indian. I know you didn't kill him."

Rafe stopped but still held the bolt gun pointed at Linda. "I might as well have," he observed sarcastically. "But for all the good it did me, I called Grandpa. I called the old pervert and asked him to get me out of the mess." Also good. Rafe was actually facing the fact that he'd now have to murder two others in order to cover up.

"Bicklin Harding was there?"

"Ahh! You'd think so. But no." There were tears forming in Rafe's eyes. "He sent a minion. Like he always does unless he wants to screw something in person."

Charlie didn't want to get him angry or make him lose focus or catch on to his right hand sawing at the leathers, so he said gently. "Please, Rafe, calm down. I know your brother would want you to think this through. If you tell me who he sent – who Liz Wallace was so afraid of – I may still be able to help you."

"That judge he buys."

Charlie had to pause for a second. This couldn't be right. "You mean Bill Wooten?"

Rafe nodded his head in agreement, then started rattling out words like an old typewriter. "When he got there he told me to call somebody we could frame. I grabbed my mom's cell phone from the office and called Liz Wallace. It was on the speed dial. I didn't even know her then. Everything after that happened so fast that I don't even know if I can remember all of it. She showed up there and started calling for my mom. She was horrified when she discovered my dad. I thought she was going to go into convulsions, she was screaming and crying so loudly. Both of us hid out in the office until we heard the Indian get there. I guess he assumed she was the murderer and figured he could put the moves on her without paying any penalty. Before me and the judge could show ourselves, she had clobbered him. That's when we showed ourselves and she ran out of there with the tire iron in her hand.

"Wooten had me gather up all the air wrenches and tire irons in the place – to confuse the cops – and I don't know what he did with them."

Rafe saw Charlie glance at Linda, and took a deep breath. "That's the last story you and your girl are going to hear." He bent over and put the bolt against Linda's head. He had two fingers on the unwieldy trigger.

"Don't shoot her!" yelled Charlie, still trying to buy time. "But if you have to shoot her, don't be a coward."

The boy hesitated and moved to point the bolt partly in Charlie's direction, then thought better of it and pointed it back at Linda, pushing the tip of the steel bolt high on her temple as he stood above her. "What do you mean coward?

You're just a bastard cop. You run and hide behind cop cars and Kevlar when the going gets rough."

"You had a beef with your father," said Charlie. "But you're killing her in cold blood. She never did anything to you. Look her in the eye when you shoot her."

Rafe fixed his eyes on Linda. Charlie was glad she had the composure under fire to look him back, with a fiery anger in her eyes. He took those moments when it would be hardest for Rafe to pull the trigger to finish getting himself loose. He took his eyes off Linda for just a moment, just enough to quickly grab a piece of splintered board to use as a crude weapon. The bolt gun went off with a loud pop of compressed air. Linda!

Chapter Twelve

When he'd first arrived in Iowa City, he hadn't expected his stay there to last for two weeks. If she didn't get out of UI Hospital that evening, it would be over two weeks. But he had no intention of leaving her – not ever. For a cop – well, an ex-cop – a woman who had cop instincts had to be either a partner or the most indispensable help mate he would ever find. The night before, getting tired of spending too much dead time alone in his motel room after visiting hours, he'd found a late-hours florist and ordered her the biggest bouquet of spring flowers he could imagine. The florist had said that size was rarely sent because of the high price. Charlie figured hang the cost. Even if he'd have to give Liz Wallace the ten grand back, nothing was too good for the woman who had saved his life. It had yet to dawn on him that, under those circumstances, it would be Linda's money paying for the flowers – and for his other surprise.

He limped up the steps to the hospital somewhat clumsily, stopping midway up to hold onto the handrail to catch his breath and steel his mind against the searing pain that bit into his left thigh. The day was extraordinarily cloudy, the first cloudy day he'd seen since arriving, and a stiff wind blew from the north – one of those normal downturns in the weather as spring struggles to turn into summer on the Great Plains. The doctor had said that the bolt was the largest object he'd ever removed from anyone outside of combat in Iraq. It would take a while for the muscle tissue to grow back and he needed a lot of physical therapy. Hang the therapy, too. When he got back to Chicago, he'd go see a real doctor – somebody who wasn't twenty years his junior. If old Doc Chervenka said he needed PT, then he would maybe consider it.

The van that scurried past the stairs to the lower level loading area of the hospital had the name of a funeral home on the side. When he'd started as a cop, all the hearses in Chicago had been Cadillac limos, even the ones they sent to the hospital morgue for the recently departed. He had no way of knowing if Iowa City had ever had a Cadillac hearse. It seemed that the further you went out west, the fewer obeisances had ever been paid to the harsh realities of life – like death. It reminded him that not everyone had made it out of that barn alive. He would have to live with it, and he could do that, as he'd done with other killings done in the line of duty. It's just that this one had seemed so personal.

On his way to the bank of elevators, he saw a young female nurse in blue scrubs who offered to go get him a wheelchair. Gritting his teeth in a forced smile, he stubbornly explained that he wasn't a patient anymore and didn't plan to be again. She smiled and said she admired his determination, but she also wouldn't fault him if he gave in to the pain. Young punk, he thought – until he realized that she had the same smiling innocence and bald-faced desire to help that he'd had when he went to Chicago Police Academy. He chastised himself as he rode to Linda's floor in the crowded car. Curmudgeon would have been a polite term for what he wanted to call himself.

He'd seen to it that Linda had a private room. And that was about all he could do except wait until they released her and he could get her back to some real Chicago doctors. She'd suffered a serious fracture to her clavicle and a shoulder dislocation that'd made him wince to see. But she'd gone through the pain and the operation like a trooper, and he hoped that – being as it was five days post-surgery – they would release her and let him drive her home.

Arnie Whittaker was there in the room when he got there. He and Linda were having an animated conversation despite the heavy cast on her right shoulder and the pain in her eyes that perhaps only Charlie could see. "Talking about me again?" he quipped as he limped through the door. He tried to avoid making himself appear to be in pain, but needed badly to sit down, and fumbled worse while trying to get settled into the only remaining chair in the room.

Whittaker looked at him with a smirk and no effort whatsoever to assist Charlie with the other chair. "Yeah, we were talking about how some old coots don't listen to their doctors."

"'Cause some old coots don't want over-the-hill police sergeants that masquerade as detectives making the moves on their girlfriends while they're listening to their doctors try to work their ways out of puberty." Charlie grinned, but the pain in his leg showed as he tried to find a comfortable position.

Linda decided she'd better change the conversation before it started to be about not enough corners to mark. "Gentlemen!" She turned to Whittaker and said, "Weren't we discussing my statement and the fact that Charlie "the Coot" Komensky won't face any charges?"

"Okay," said Whittaker. His face took on a serious expression. "The first part of your statement is clear. Rafe Flatwood confessed to the murder of his father twice. Once when he bound you up and threw you into the barn, and again after he brought Charlie in and tied him to a chair. He was also in possession of a bolt gun – operated by compressed air and modified so that it didn't hold the bolt captive. And that appears to be the murder weapon. That can be confirmed by ballistics.

"So when you had the opportunity, you followed Komensky's lead and picked up a piece of scrap and used it to saw at your bindings whenever Flatwood was distracted. Am I right so far?"

Linda nodded, but she was looking at Charlie and smiling broadly at him. Charlie smiled back and reached over to hold her good hand while Whittaker continued. "So when you believed you had communicated the fact that both of you were nearly free, and it looked like Flatwood was getting out of control, Flatwood realized that Komensky was getting loose. When he pointed the bolt gun at Komensky's head, you threw him off balance rising up and butting him with your shoulder. You realized that you had failed to keep him from shooting the bolt at Komensky when you heard a blood-curdling cry, but by then Flatwood had recovered himself enough to kick you hard, resulting in your broken bones.

Flatwood then went at you and dislocated your arm trying to drag you to his truck.

"It was at this time you saw that Komensky was bleeding profusely but he was coming at Flatwood with the splintered two-by. But Komensky was going to use it as a club and strike Flatwood across the back, which he did, not causing any apparently fatal injury. This is when a hand-to-hand took place between Komensky and Flatwood, which appeared to end when Flatwood kicked Komensky's bloody injured leg and the pain caused him to lose his balance and fall backward. You saw Flatwood moving to jump in top of Komensky and, at the same time, Komensky got the big splinter into his right hand, pointed end up, and he was on his back?"

Linda nodded again. "That's right," she said. "And that's when I saw that I was near the air hose and I just yanked it up into the air with my good arm to trip Flatwood. I expected to trip him, but that's not what happened." This time she looked up at Charlie as if to say she was sorry.

Whittaker continued, "So Flatwood gets tangled up in the hose, and, with a full head of steam, he goes face first into the giant splinter, which is wedged just hard enough into the dry dirt floor to offer resistance."

"If it makes any difference," Charlie said with raised eyebrows. "I don't think he felt as much pain as I was feeling at that moment. It was over pretty fast. We found our cell phones in the big Hummer, along with another rifle for you to match with any slugs you may recover from the Frederickson shooting, and a trick-shot sling that fit to a hook in the head liner. Link Sheffield was the lucky one. Apart from the hangover he had the next day, he didn't come out of it until the ambulances got there, and he didn't have to witness any of the bloodshed."

Linda seemed to go into a pensive mood. "What happens now?" she asked Whittaker.

"For one thing, Liz Wallace is going to have to stand trial for manslaughter," he answered. "We arrested Judge Wooten, but he made bail almost faster than we could process him. He might turn, though, when he finds out that Bicklin Harding won't be in any kind of a position to help him out. Young Danny is singing like a canary. I expect that both his grandfather and his mother will stand trial for criminal sexual penetration and child abuse. Sheffield's financial situation isn't going to get any better, either. He'll be facing at least one count of conspiracy.

"Meanwhile, back at the courthouse, Sharedream's family is filing a big lawsuit against Trapp Tire, although it won't be worth much if the company goes bankrupt. It's CEO has already been thrown out of her office and replaced, and Margaret Trapp will probably also stand for conspiracy or obstruction."

Charlie interrupted. "Did you get the part where Rafe Flatwood said he just grabbed the big screw you found in his father's head from a box? I still don't know how he did that without putting fingerprints on it?"

"Have you ever done any heavy wood-frame work?"

Whittaker's question was serious and made Linda laugh. "Have you ever seen Charlie try to use a set of tools?"

All three of them enjoyed the joke, and then Whittaker explained, "Those heavy screws bind pretty hard in big timber, even when there are pilot holes like in the racks Danny Senior was building. So the screw factory packs them with plastic sleeves over the threads so they don't get nicked and become impossible to twist.

"Don't be too hard on your guy," he said to Linda. "I didn't know that, either. We didn't find any sleeves at the scene, so nobody thought of it. I guess that's just one more thing that Wooten covered up. We'll find them, though. It's just a matter of time."

Charlie stood up and winced. "My leg's killing me and it's just a matter of time before I go crazy if we don't get back to Chicago soon. But there's one more thing I need to do before I go, and I'm going to need a witness." He turned to Whittaker and said, "So a hick cop from a two-bit Iowa town will have to do."

"I'm listening," said Whittaker.

Linda, too, was now watching Charlie, so, with a flourish, he took a small padded box out of his right pocket and handed it to Linda. "Is this what I think it is?" she asked, looking up at him with a sly smile.

"Open it."

In the box, she found an engagement ring hammered out of the piece of steel she had used to cut her leather bonds. In the makeshift setting sat a piece of glass from a shattered barn window. Whoever had made it had put grooves into the circumference that looked like tire treads.

Charlie smiled a big, wide smile and winked. "The jeweler next door to Sheffield's does custom orders on short notice. And he doesn't like Sheffield's neon sign, either. Now let's get the future Mrs. Komensky released so we can get the hell out of here."

Epilogue

Located in the east central part of the state, Iowa City is the former capital of the Iowa Territory and first capital of the State of Iowa. It has a current population of just under 68,000 souls and is the home of the University of Iowa. It is served by two freight railroads, Iowa Interstate Railroad, and Cedar Rapids and Iowa City Railway, but currently has no passenger rail service. Thus, Charlie could not have taken the train to Iowa City as he was wont to do.

On the way out to Iowa City by car, Charlie may have stopped in Rock Island, Illinois, the namesake city for the old Chicago, Rock Island and Pacific, which went bankrupt in 1980 and was shut down and liquidated. He would have enjoyed an excursion to the Silvis, Illinois, shop complex that has subsequently been the site of locomotive and railcar remanufacture and production.

If he had thought about it, and considering how much he would eventually wind up having to pay for car rental – those deductibles mount up when somebody blows up your rental – he could have taken the California Zephyr to Ottumwa, Iowa, and rented a car there to drive to Iowa City.

Charlie enjoyed his visit with the train crew on the Cedar Rapids and Iowa City (CRANDIC). This fascinating little railroad was once all electric and had fast passenger service in electric cars between its end-point cities. It ceased passenger operation in 1953, and now offers diesel freight switching for customers along its approximately sixty mile length. Through freight is handled by other railroads with rights to run along its line.

The electric railroad in Mason City is one of the few remnants of the vast network of electric interurban railways that strung together smaller towns in Midwest and Eastern Plains states. Charlie postponed his investigation to savor the sound of electric motors geared to the locomotive wheels and the smell of ozone produced by sparks where the trolley pole contacts the hot electric overhead wire. But if he had not stayed that long, he would never have had the opportunity to see what his client and Margaret Trapp were up to.

Charlie has never thought much of the railfan environment of Des Moines. Although it is the state capital, Des Moines doesn't have any passenger rail service, the nearest Amtrak station being in Osceola, about forty miles south. However, he would have enjoyed poking around the industrial sidings near the Trapp Tire distribution center, if he'd had the time, and imagining a time when the electric interurban served Des Moines, as well.

With Charlie's car in the shop being dried out from its unscheduled dunking, and Linda unable to drive her car back to Oak Brook, perhaps the newly engaged couple will think twice and book a couple of seats on the next eastbound Zephyr for a romantic train ride back into Chicago.

Then again, Linda doesn't like trains as much as Detective Charlie Komensky.

Watch for the second Charlie Komensky mystery –

Secondary Smoke: The Steam Locomotive Murders

on Pagination Books.

Other Books by Charles A. Turek

The Plutonium Standard

A Tunnel Too Far

The Acceleration of Time

207

www.ingramcontent.com/pod-product-compliance
Lightning Source LLC
Chambersburg PA
CBHW070829120626
46556CB00002B/689